Invitation
To
Murder

INVITATION TO MURDER

Ralph Trevor

RAMBLE HOUSE

2018

First American trade paperback edition

Ramble House
10329 Sheephead Drive
Vancleave MS 39565 USA

www.ramblehouse.com

ISBN 13: 978-1-60543-950-1

Preparation: Gavin L. O'Keefe
Cover design & introduction © 2018 Gavin L. O'Keefe

About the author

JAMES REGINALD WILMOT was born in Birkenhead, Cheshire, England in 1897, and died in Wirral, Cheshire in 1944. His was an early passing; any further information about Wilmot's life is elusive. What we do know is that in his brief writing career (from 1935 to 1944) Wilmot wrote at least thirty-one mystery novels under the pseudonym 'Ralph Trevor' and eight romantic novels under the 'Frances Stewart' by-line.

The author's sole publisher appears to have been Wright & Brown, London, the stalwart firm who issued so many books in the 1930s and '40s for (primarily) the lending library market. W&B built up a stable of authors who could reliably turn out novels in the most popular genres of the day: mysteries, thrillers, romance, adventure and 'air mysteries.' Amongst those authors were Gerald Verner, Roland Daniel, Jack Mann[1] and John G. Brandon—writers still remembered today for their many crime and thriller novels. Other authors published by W&B have not been remembered so well: Mary Richmond, Rex Dark, Phillip Condé, Gwyn Evans and Louis Kaye.[2]

Wilmot seems to have fallen midway between the two groups of W&B authors listed above. While not terribly well-known under his most prolifically-used pseudonym Ralph Trevor, his many books released under that name are yet sought after by connoisseurs in their original W&B editions.

Though modest compared with other authors' works in the genre, the Ralph Trevor mystery novels still hold up well—they feature memorable characters and are written with 'style'—and they deserve to be brought back into print for a 21st century audience. It is hoped that this new series of Ramble House reprints will be a positive move in that direction.

---

1. Pseudonym of Charles Henry Cannell (1882-1947), *aka* E. Charles Vivian. The 'Jack Mann' pseudonym was used for the 'Gees' series of supernatural detective novels and several other works.
2. Ramble House has reprinted novels (originally published by W&B) by Gerald Verner, Roland Daniel, Jack Mann, John G. Brandon, Rex Dark, Phillip Condé and Ralph Trevor, thus doing its bit to revive these writers and their works.

Contemporary ad included in W&B books

JAMES REGINALD WILMOT
BIBLIOGRAPHY

Novels by 'Ralph Trevor'

On the Night of the Ninth	1935
The Eyes through the Mask	1935
The Moorcroft Manor Mystery	1935
The House of Silence	1935
Some Person Unknown	1935
The Monday Night Murder	1935
Invitation to Murder	1936
Under Suspicion	1936
Death in the Surgery	1937
Murder in Silk	1937
Murder Without Regret	1937
The Ghost Counts Ten	1938
The Deputy Avenger	1938
Death Burns the Candle	1938
Viper's Vengeance	1938
Death Comes Too Late	1938
The Corpse in the Caravan	1939
Easy for the Crook	1939
Murder for Two Pins	1939
The Ace of Clubs Murder	1939
Sky-High Terror	1940
The Girl in the Crimson Cloak	1940
Meet Doctor Death	1940
Behind the Green Mask	1940
Murder in the Fifth Column	1940

Who Killed the Crooner?	1941
The Phantom Raider	1941
Red Strands for Danger	1941
A Murder has been Arranged	1942
High Spy	1942
Front Page Murder	1942

Novels by 'Frances Stewart'

The Flame was Crimson	1938
Sweet Avenger	1938
Paradise of Dreams	1939
Such Love is Dangerous	1939
For Love and Money	1940
Love Enters the Picture	1940
Love Takes the Stage	1943
Love is a Patient Thing	1944

CHAPTER ONE

THE LETTER

FROM THE BREAKFAST-room at Blacon Grange it was possible to see the wonderful avenue of copper beeches that flanked the winding, grey drive. They had been sturdy fellows when Cromwell had been knocking about the county, creating the ruins for the benefit of present-day antiquarians. From that you will gather that Blacon Grange had something of a past.

On this autumn morning John Vance, having completed his appreciation of the bronzed panorama away over the sweep of the lawns, turned to the neat pile of correspondence beside his plate at the breakfast-table. Although he had retired three or four years ago from the stockbroking business which had provided him with a not inconsiderable share of this world's wealth, he had found it impossible to cut himself adrift completely from the hazards of speculation. As he occasionally phrased it, "If one has to have a hobby, why not let it be business?" Which explains why there should have been that little pile of correspondence on the breakfast-table of a man who had dropped into the guise of a country gentleman with the easy nonchalance of accepted tradition.

At fifty-five John Vance still retained the dominant personality that had made him a name in city circles. Nature had fashioned him well. She had given him a face that was strong in every line from forehead to chin. There was no suggestion of loose flesh about it; nothing that betokened individual indulgence. The chin was round and firm; the nose long and straight with narrow nostrils, while the eyes, intensely blue and exceptionally clear, were surmounted by heavy eye-brows which, like the hair, were somewhat greyer than they had a right to be.

Almost idly his fingers roamed through the little pile of oddly assorted envelopes. He was not particularly in the mood for work this morning; he wanted to go down to the stables and unhitch White Wanderer from her stall and go for a gallop with Pamela over the slowly dying bracken on the Common towards Fenstope and back again through Much Wendor, where some of the streets were still cobbled just as they had been two hundred years ago. After all, he considered, there couldn't be anything very urgent; share certificates to be signed; a bond to be endorsed; a letter most likely from Cooks', who were fixing up a ten-weeks' tour in Upper Egypt. All of them could wait quite well until nearer lunch time.

He strode back again to the window and looked at his watch. Pamela was late. It was nine o'clock, and she knew how he hated being kept waiting for breakfast. Yet in his heart he also knew that he could never be really angry with Pamela. She was all he had—all he ever would have. Back again to the table his eyes rested on the correspondence again. The little stack had fallen sideways, fanning themselves out somewhat like a pack of playing-cards, and it was then that he saw one envelope that arrested his attention. Most of them were either typewritten or else written in that rather larger, scrawling calligraphy which most people use when addressing envelopes. But this one was *printed*—printed in red ink. Immediately interested, he picked it up and scrutinised it further. It was rather careless printing, he thought . . . as though it had been done hurriedly. . . .

> JOHN VANCE, ESQUIRE,
> BLACON GRANGE,
> BLACON,
> HEREFORDSHIRE.

The post-mark was plain enough. The letter had been posted in London at seven o'clock the previous evening—posted in the Strand.

Just then the door of the breakfast-room was flung open and Pamela appeared, penitent but very gay.

"So sorry to be late, Daddy. I suppose you've been waiting ages?"

Pamela flung her arms around her father's neck and kissed him. It was a morning ritual whenever they were together, and on those occasions when Pamela was not home for breakfast John Vance had to admit that something was missing from his life.

"Any mail for me?" she asked, looking quickly around the breakfast-table. "No? Ah, well, I detest replying to letters, and fortunately most of my friends are well aware of my weaknesses."

Pamela Vance presented a picture of vibrant health. At twenty-five she possessed all the old vitality of her father. The eager light of action sparkled in the clear, crystal-blue pools of her eyes; the complete face was one of animation and action. She was of the type and the temperament that wanted urgently to get things done. When ideas occurred to her there was no rest until they had become accomplishments. Sometimes, perhaps, she regretted an impetuosity, but the regret had been only momentary; it had lost itself in the next urgent desire; the next thing waiting to be done. And it is said of those who possess blue eyes and dark hair that they have the temperament of Pamela Vance.

Vance rang for the meal to be served, still holding in his hand the envelope addressed in red ink that had intrigued him a moment ago.

"Anything important, Daddy? Hope it won't interfere with our jog-trot. Remember, you promised to take me over to Foxholes?" Pamela had pulled out a chair and began munching a finger of crisp brown toast.

"I haven't forgotten," smiled her father. "There's nothing I would let interfere with a promise made to you."

Vance followed his daughter's example and seated himself.

Birtles brought in the breakfast under gleaming silver covers.

" 'Morning, Birtles," greeted the girl. "Mrs. Marston in good form this morning?"

"I think so, Miss Pamela. The kidney looks inviting."

"Good. We'll get busy!"

Vance had slit the mysterious envelope and had pulled out a single sheet of plain notepaper. Pamela was busying herself before a serving dish containing an appetising selection of Mrs. Marston's early morning form.

"Two slices of bacon, Daddy? Or is it three?" she inquired without looking up.

For the space of a split second there was silence, but it was long enough to cause the girl to look up quickly.

"What was that, my dear? Bacon, did you say? I—stupid of me, of course. Yes, dear, two—yes, two."

"What's the matter?" asked Pamela shrewdly. "Bad news?"

Vance smiled. "I really don't know," he replied with a curious smile. "It's rather odd."

"What's odd?"

"Don't let's talk about it," he suggested, reaching for the bread. "It's probably nothing at all—just a joke. It can't be serious, can it?"

Almost before he had finished speaking, Pamela had pushed back her chair and was beside him. He was still holding the sheet of letter paper in his hand and she saw that that hand was trembling.

"Please," the girl requested, taking the letter from his unresisting fingers and gazing at what was scrawled there.

Dear Sir,

You are probably aware that the debt of honour has not yet been paid. It is necessary in the interests of Society that Martin Stone be sent to oblivion. We give you three days in which to accomplish the death of this enemy. Failing this . . . you know the penalty. Remember the S.P.M.

The letter was unsigned.

John Vance gazed absently across the breakfast-table as his daughter read the strange letter beside him. He did not quite know what his eyes were seeing. All he knew was that the wheels of Time were beginning to revolve in his tumult of a mind and, what is more, they were revolving backwards.

The wheels stopped suddenly, and the reason for the cessation was that Pamela was laughing loudly, disturbing the dramatic poise of his thoughts; destroying the mainspring of madness. The tension was snapping in her laugh, and he wanted to laugh too.

"As a practical joke I suppose it infringes the laws of good taste," laughed the girl, "but this is the first time I've ever heard of anyone being told to commit murder. I suppose that's what it means."

"It certainly looks like it," Vance told her, and his tone was still hesitant. "I suppose it *is* queer."

"Your breakfast's getting cold," Pamela warned him, practically. "You'd better have some fresh bacon."

Her father waved a protesting hand. "Just a cup of coffee," he said, "and make it strong."

The girl made no comment as she poured out the hot beverage. A joke might be a joke, but John Vance had never drunk coffee before his bacon until this morning.

CHAPTER TWO

IAN IS JEALOUS

IAN GRENVILLE LOOKED every inch of him the perfect country gentleman. He was tall, rather slim in build, and his hair was almost flaxen. For how many generations the Grenvilles had been considerably south of the Tweed he did not know, but somewhere in the distant past there had been an ancestor on the female side who had sported the title of lowland chieftain somewhere in the vicinity of Roxburghshire. It was no doubt from this veteran of the Border raids that Ian had inherited his bearing and, to no inconsiderable degree, his fighting spirit.

At twenty-six, unlike some of the more modern young men of his acquaintance, he had no ambition to go to business in the City, while the lives led by the rubber and tea planters in distant corners of the Empire held no glamour for him. He had never felt the pioneer urge so close to the heart of Mr. Kipling. England was good enough for him. He loved the land; loved the countryside; felt that it was good to tramp through the russet bracken and the heather; good to climb Pingery Tump when the wind sang lyrics through the rowan trees and scythed through the short, thin-fingered grasses that carpeted the slopes of the hill.

Colonel Sir John Grenville, his father, held a small estate to the eastward of Blacon village, and now its management was in the hands of Ian. He had come down from Cambridge at twenty-one, and for five years he had been making himself commendably proficient in the routine work of estate management, which had been necessary since Sir John's disablement as a result of war service in Flanders. It was pleasant work. The three farms, thanks to scientific management, were quite flourishing concerns, and the tenants had a high regard for the young man who had so quickly dispelled any misgivings they may have harboured about the utility of a graduate from the History School at Cambridge.

The young man had just completed his round of the farms and had decided to walk over to Hereford to inspect a new milk churn. It was a stiff ten-mile walk, but Ian preferred that to his two-seater, which he strictly reserved for longer journeys and for less clement weather.

His way led past the foot of Pingery Tump, the little humped-back hill that stood out in the landscape as though it had been accidentally left behind when Nature was tired of moving the mountains that lay westward. On the higher ground to the north was a rough-clad plateau from which one could glimpse Blacon village, nestling in the green and brown folds below.

He strode forward briskly, dressed as usual in his rough brown tweeds and tweed soft hat with the brim permanently turned down. In one corner of his mouth was a well-smoked briar.

The wind was keen, but the sunshine that accompanied it tempered the razor-like edge of it. A few sheep grazing on the higher levels were the only living things visible to the eye. To Ian Grenville this was life; real, vibrant life, far removed from the artificiality which bred so many perplexing problems. It made him think that Nature in her wisdom knew best what was good for man. The soil held the secret of Life—a greater secret than the one for which the scientists toiled to solve in their elaborate laboratories, and yet one which needed no solution.

So went his thoughts once again as he jogged at a pleasant trot down the hill towards the winding bridle track that led to Foxholes, a bracken-cloaked hollow where, in due season, motoring picnic parties were wont to gather during the summer week-ends.

It was only then that he was jolted from philosophic thoughts at the sight of two riders cantering down the slopes from the westward. The vision of them caused a quickening of his heart-beats, for there was only one woman he knew could sit a horse with such grace and such aplomb in the canter, and that woman was Pamela Vance. She was riding her dappled grey, a beautiful hunter which had more than once "done itself proud," as they said in Blacon, at the Point-to-Point. Ian himself had advised John Vance to purchase the horse at the autumn sales a year ago, and although he had never been entered for a race since Pamela had become his owner, he did not seem to mind the derating in the least.

Pamela caught sight of the figure bearing down upon them and waved a gay hand in greeting, and Ian returned the salute with joyous alacrity. This was rare luck—a slice of luck he had never expected, because John Vance and his daughter almost invariably rode before breakfast.

The young man's heart was still pounding within him—beating an excited tattoo composed by the oldest composer in the world—Love. Yes, Mr. Ian Grenville was very much in love with Pamela Vance—so much in love with her that there were occasions when he was apt to become mysteriously temperamental, an emotion to which the Grenvilles as a family were not particularly prone.

He watched the girl spur the animal into a gallop, leaving her father to jog-trot behind. He watched the hooves kicking up little flecks of brown earth with rhythmic regularity.

"Hello, Ian!" she greeted him as she reined in the dapple-grey. "We're late this morning, but it was quite my fault. My bed was more comfortable than it had any right to be on so glorious a morning. And where may you be going?"

"Just over to Hereford," he told her. "No need to inquire where you're going," he added, nodding in the direction of Foxholes. "Wish I was coming with you," regretfully.

"Men must work," she chided him, with a dimpled smile.

Just then John Vance drew up alongside his daughter.

"Good morning, young man."

"Good morning, sir," acknowledged Ian. "A fine morning for blowing away dull care."

"Daddy hasn't a care in the world," interposed the girl, so swiftly that Ian glanced quickly into her face. "Have you, Daddy?"

A curious smile came to John Vance's lips. Pamela was always one for stepping swiftly into the breach, and it would certainly not do, he thought, to talk about the strange letter he had received that morning.

"I suppose not," he confessed, a trifle more dully than he might otherwise have done, "but I've had them in plenty in my time, young fellow, and sometimes it's rather difficult to break the habit."

Pamela laughed happily, but she was wondering why Ian Grenville had made such a singularly inept remark. It was foolish to imagine that he knew anything about the mystery.

For a moment the trio remained silent—the kind of silence that occasionally comes between people meeting together unexpectedly, but before conversation could be remade there was a diversion. From the direction in which the young man had come a third rider was approaching. For a moment he was silhouetted on the skyline and then, apparently having seen his objective, pushed his mount into a gallop—a dangerous gallop down the hill towards them.

It was Pamela who saw him first, and Ian was quick to notice the change that came over the girl's features. A new light danced in her eyes: the wind flush on her cheeks deepened.

"Here's Rodney," she exclaimed, "and he looks like coming to a particularly nasty end if he rides often like he's doing now."

Ian turned and watched the rider almost tumbling towards them from the edge of the plateau, seemingly without a care either for himself or his horse.

Rodney Delisle seemed to reach the group in less time than it had taken for Pamela to draw attention to him. For the last hundred yards the unfortunate animal, on a tight rein, almost slithered on his haunches, a procedure that brought an angry glow to young Ian Grenville's face.

The newcomer was a man whose age was probably between thirty and thirty-five. He was stockily built and the possessor of an almost olive complexion. His clean-cut features gave him a handsome cast of countenance, and his grooming told a story of visits to Savile Row and the emporiums of the best tailors in the world. His riding suit was immaculate and faultlessly cut and, not without a trace of amusement, Ian noted that the fellow's riding boots were actually spurred. The only note that seemed oddly out of keeping was that he was hatless, but that, Ian persuaded himself, was solely for the purpose of revealing how sleek black hair can be brushed into an unalterable position despite the elements.

"I called at the house," he explained when greetings were over, "and they told me you had come along this way, so I whisked out the old charger and here I am. I want freshening up, and I know of no better way than a good gallop in pleasant company. What say you, Grenville?"

"You'll break your neck and your horse a fetlock if you ride as you just have done," said Ian. "As to your other sentiments, I'm with you every time. Only wish I could get a mount out and come with you. But I've got business to attend to," he added, slyly malicious.

"I'm afraid we're keeping you from your appointment, Ian," suggested Pamela. "See you again soon, I hope."

"Mustn't keep the world's workers from their work, must we?" echoed Delisle, displaying his teeth in a smile. "Well, cheerio, Grenville."

Ian Grenville smiled, but there was bitterness in his heart. "You're not keeping me," he said to Pamela. "It's nice to see you in the saddle occasionally. You ride so remarkably well—a born horsewoman, I should say."

"Flatterer," laughed the girl. "Well, good-bye, Ian."

"Good-bye, Pamela!"

He stood and watched them move off towards Foxholes, and his hands were tightly clenched. He was wondering what Pamela could ever see in that bounder Delisle—wondering, too, whether she really did prefer Delisle's company to his own.

It didn't do to lay too much store by village gossip, but one couldn't help hearing it now and again, and it was said down in Blacon that Rodney Delisle's "affair" with Pamela Vance was making very nice progress and that there would be wedding bells at St. Christopher's before the year was out. All of which stung Ian Grenville deeply. He was in love with Pamela, yet she would not let him tell her so. Once she had said that she would never marry while her father lived, that there was far too great an attachment between them for anything like that to happen, and yet it was common knowledge that Rodney Delisle, who twelve months ago had taken a house not far from Blacon Grange, was making "nice progress!"

Could it be that, despite Pamela's assertion, gossip was right? It certainly looked as if it were. He remembered the look that had come into the girl's face as she recognised Delisle in the distance. He was certain its replica had not been there when she had first caught sight of him.

Away towards the road tramped the young man, but there was no spring in his step. The riders had become lost to view among the trees to the north. Then he thought about John Vance. How quiet he had been—and how Pamela had interposed quickly when the remark about dull care had been made. Coming to think of it, it was decidedly odd. John Vance was usually a rather happily communicative man, and he had not been so this morning. Looking back on the encounter, the young man began to feel that there was something amiss—something perhaps that accounted for the lateness of the ride. The new train of thought refreshed him; it helped to obliterate the cynical smile he had seen on Rodney Delisle's thin lips as he had ridden away beside Pamela. The idea of wealthy John Vance with so much as a speck of care in the world was really rather ludicrous, and yet he certainly had not appeared to be his usual smiling self that morning, and Pamela—yes, Pamela—appeared rather overstrung; rather forced, in fact . . . until Delisle turned up!

"Oh, hell!" he grumbled, petulantly. "What's the use of being in love?"

CHAPTER THREE

MARTIN STONE TELEPHONES

SOON AFTER THE arrival of Delisle John Vance made an excuse to return to Blacon Grange alone. Pamela, of course, had protested because she, and she alone, knew what was on her father's mind. Despite her laughing protestations that the affair of the letter was little more than an absurd practical joke, she had experienced a touch of the sinister about it. All the morning during their ride she had striven to defeat the thought. More than once she had laughed almost out loud at her morbid fears. Yet behind all her common sense there was a suspicion of haunting fear.

John Vance smiled at his daughter's protest. He knew what was in her mind for a certainty. She was worrying about him, and as for himself . . . John Vance did not know what to think.

Having handed his horse over to the groom, Vance went to his study and slumped heavily into a chair beside the fire. To the cautious observer the man's face appeared to have grown older in the past few hours—older and more grey. He might also have been able to accept his daughter's estimate of the whole affair, had it not been for those rather ominous initials which the letter contained.

He took the missive from his letter-case and read it over for the twentieth time.

"Remember the S.P.M."

Those words took his mind back thirty years. The kaleidoscopic panorama of the Past reversed, He was back again in San Luis—a young man enthusiastic with all the wild, sometimes impossible, enthusiasms of youth. Even in those days he had been something of an idealist. He had gone out with a stern belief in the New World. He had trecked across America—a seeker after fortune—and he had landed in San Luis in the height of his adventurous enthusiasm. In some ways success measured in terms of the dollar came easily, and in San Luis he had a reputation for honesty and industry.

In those days in San Luis there were a number of young men—the majority of them British by birth or extraction— stimulated by similar ideals. They used to meet together at week-ends and discuss life and love and all those things that young men *do* discuss when they are together. And one of the things they discussed was the future of Mexico. All of them had unbounded faith in the country. Unlike the United States, it was comparatively undeveloped, but in the process of development that was forecast for the next decade they saw a danger. They saw Mexico becoming a prey to all that was worst in American life. They saw the beginnings of graft.

In order to combat this sinister thing they formed themselves into a society. They felt (as most Britishers instinctively do when they are domiciled abroad) that the Mexicans were inadequately equipped mentally and morally for the task of preventing their country from becoming undermined by political and industrial sedition. In that belief there was formed an organisation with the imposing (and rather absurd) title "The Society for the Purification of Mexico." Vance could not remember just now just who it was invented that insignia, but it did not matter very much. Equally imposing rules were drawn up, and the handful of members were sworn, in the midst of a fantastic rite, not only to secrecy, but also to obedience.

The new society imposed on its members certain obligations, and in the oath of allegiance each member had to swear that at all times and under all circumstances he must be ready and willing to carry out such tasks, (whether they be inside or outside the law was of no consequence) as the High Council should command.

Often times in the past he had recalled the absurdity. So far as he knew no one had been called on to fulfil his pledge. Yet not all had joined that society with high ideals. Two men, perhaps a third, had scented advantage to themselves in the idealism of others. There had been murder done—not for the sake of high ideals, not for the sake of Mexico—but for that very material advantage, taken at whatever cost, against which the society had brought itself into being.

They had escaped in the turbulence of the times. There had been no trial. But they had betrayed the harmless little society to those who read a great deal more into its silly little rules than was intended, and its members were at once proscribed and forced to flee from Mexico. A sudden change of government, not unaccompanied by somewhat extravagant bloodshed, had spared the scattered members from any harassment of the law, but at the back of his mind Vance always had the disturbing, indeed ugly, thought, that in the eyes of the law he was the accomplice, unwilling and un-knowing, of two murderers.

He had gone north from Mexico to New York and Wall Street. He had lost touch with the Brothers. Treachery had disbanded their society and idealism had vanished before the grossest materialism. No one would remember (or having remembered, would not im-mediately put the thought out of his head) any more the scene or subject of the society, and certainly no one was any longer liable to fulfil the pledge.

Five years after he had left Mexico a chance encounter with one of his former colleagues gave him the information that both the traitors had died in a minor revolution on the Mexican border. Not once since had he seen anyone or heard anything at all even re-motely connected with that episode in the past. Yet that third man—vaguely down the avenues of his mind he tried to trace what he could remember of him. Not from that day when they left Mexico until this had he heard anything of him, nor had he more than mere intuition to persuade him that the man was a traitor with the other two. If he or any others of that society had been in Eng-land, Vance felt that sooner or later he would have heard from them. For many years the name of John Vance was too well-known in London and the provinces to escape notice. A successful financier seldom can fail to escape publicity. But none had claimed knowledge of those early Mexican days, and until today the matter had gone from his mind.

There was one thing, he decided: no one must ever know that he had been so foolish as to ally himself to so ridiculous a cause, and what was more, he had not the least intention of availing himself of the anonymous correspondent's invitation to remove from this world Mr. Martin Stone.

A command to murder! After thirty years or more had come this strange message. It seemed fantastic. He wanted to laugh; felt that laughter was the correct antidote for the situation and yet . . . who was there left with knowledge of that youthful society; who was it who now demanded fulfilment of the pledge?

It was odd, he thought suddenly, that the subject for the murder should have been Martin Stone. Odd, too, that one of the last deals he had made before his retirement from the City should have been with Martin Stone. That had been two years ago. He remembered it now clearly. There had been some trouble over the deal. Stone, it was alleged, had misrepresented certain blocks of shares which were on offer. At least that was how it had appeared at the time, and

Vance remembered that Stone had been rather unpleasant about it. He had, in fact, suggested that Vance had agreed to take up the shares as part of the deal when Vance had declared that the transaction had never been mentioned.

The matter had been straightened out, but not before a certain amount of bad feeling had been engendered between the two firms, and Vance, feeling that he himself had acted as an honest financier, had certainly had no qualms of conscience and had not pursued the matter further. From that day he had not heard from Martin Stone and knew nothing of him except obliquely that he was still in business.

Pamela came in in the midst of his recollections, bringing Delisle with her.

"I hope you don't mind, Daddy," she said, as she sat on the broad arm of his chair, "but I've been telling Rodney about that silly letter you had this morning and he agrees with me that someone is playing a practical joke on you; don't you, Roddy?"

Rodney Delisle laughed. "Good lord, yes! I've never heard of anything so utterly ridiculous. You don't mean to suggest, sir, that you are taking it seriously?"

"I don't know what to think," Vance smiled. "It's such an odd thing, you know, and . . . well, just a little bit disturbing."

"You shouldn't really be worrying your head about it, Daddy," interposed Pamela, "but if you're going to go grey about it, the best thing to do is to send the letter to Scotland Yard. Roddy says that they get shoals by almost every post from people who have got the wind-up."

"That's true, sir," broke in Delisle. "I believe they've got a department doing nothing else all day long but inquiring into anonymous correspondence. Most of the letters, I've heard, are traced to lunatics who should really be under lock and key. It's more than likely that your screed comes from a similar source."

John Vance smiled as he shook his head.

"It's kind of you to be optimistic, Delisle," he said, "and I only wish I could share your optimism. I will admit, quite frankly, I'm worried. It may, of course, be just as you say. If I were younger I'd probably think the same, but I'm not. I'm getting old, and old people are a prey to suspicions. They can't help it. They see danger often where no danger really exists. I suppose it is in some curious way connected with the fear of death. I can't define it in any other way."

Pamela jumped up from her perch on the arm of her father's chair.

"We're getting morbid," she laughed. "Let's have lunch. There's nothing like food for chasing away depression. Staying, Roddy? Do say 'Yes,' and I'll have another place laid."

"Thanks—awfully," accepted Delisle. "Now you come to mention it I remember I've had no breakfast. I think we all need cheering up, don't we?"

"I'll send Birtles in with cocktails," announced the girl as she left the two men together.

~ ~ ~ ~ ~

It was midway through the following morning that the telephone bell rang.

Pamela was out riding again. Delisle had called for her shortly after breakfast and Vance was alone. As chance would have it he was crossing the hall when the instrument demanded an answer.

"Is that Blacon Two-Nine?" came the voice of the operator. "Just hold the line a moment. London wants you."

Vance held on and almost immediately came another voice—a man's voice.

"I want to speak to Mr. Vance—Mr. John Vance."

"This is Mr. Vance speaking."

"This is Martin Stone, broker," came back the voice. "I wonder if you're too busy to come down to see me this evening? I'd make it earlier if I could, but I'm going out of town almost immediately and I won't be back much before six-thirty. How would seven o'clock suit you—at my office. You know the address!"

John Vance felt his head swimming and heard himself answering that he would go up to London that evening as Stone suggested—heard the man answer a curt "Good!" and then, just as Vance was about to say something, the line became lifeless.

Furiously Vance called the operator.

"Can you give me the Exchange and number of the call I have just had?" he asked with a tremor. "It's important. I must know it!"

"If you hold the line a minute," came back the operator's voice. Silence.

"It was City 08798."

Vance picked up the London telephone directory from its hook above the table on which the instrument stood and wildly turned over its pages. Tremblingly his finger ran down the "S" column. Then it paused.

Yes, that was right.

That was Martin Stone's office number!

CHAPTER FOUR

PAMELA HAS A PROPOSAL

JOHN VANCE HAD no intention of telling anyone, not even Pamela, about that telephone conversation he had had with Martin Stone. Further than that, neither was it his intention to take Pamela to London with him on his mysterious journey, and yet the girl must be got out of the way somehow.

As it so happened, Pamela solved the problem for him at lunch time when she announced that Delisle had invited her to go with him to Hereford to meet a party of friends who were lunching there on their way by road to Holyhead. She had no idea what time she would be returning because Delisle had suggested going part of the way with his friends in his car. That meant tea in Shrewsbury.

Vance offered no objection. She was not to worry about him in the least. He even suggested that he might run over to Gloucester and have a look around. In any event he would be quite all right.

Little more had been said since yesterday about the letter, and for that Vance had been thankful. He had already spent a restless night, which had been punctuated by vivid dreams through which a succession of strange scarlet-hooded figures perambulated with devastating monotony. No one had been more glad to see the silver glimmer of the dawn than John Vance.

Strive as he would, however, throughout the day, he could not bring his mind to desert the subject of Martin Stone. He had planned the interview in its entirety. Once having found what Stone wanted with him, Vance intended to show him the letter and ask the man's advice. He might even be tempted towards facetiousness and inquire when, where and how he would like to be killed. That would, at least, bring a touch of novelty to the grotesquerie of the situation and, having done that much, there the matter—so far as Martin Stone was concerned—would end. What followed—if indeed anything would follow—was entirely a matter for the future. If, as he shrewdly suspected, there was someone still living with a knowledge of that outrageous society in San Luis, then it would be

24

for that person to make the next move. He had no intention of mentioning the matter to Scotland Yard or even at the police station at Blacon village.

Vance found that there was a train from Gloucester at three-fifteen which would get him into London shortly after six o'clock with plenty of time to get to Smith Street, E.C., where the offices of Mr. Martin Stone were situated.

While the train thundered eastwards Pamela Vance and Rodney Delisle were taking tea together in a Shrewsbury hotel.

"I suppose I can't hope that you've made up your mind, Pamela?" he asked, leaning slightly forward over the glass top of the little wickerwork table.

"A woman's mind is never made up, Roddy. It's perpetually in a state of flux," she smiled. "Daddy used to say that a woman's mind is like the Stock Market, steady enough for a day or two and then goes all to pieces."

"A kind of speculation, is that what you mean?" Pamela thought there was just the merest hint of cynicism in the man's tone.

"That's it. Not a particularly good investment, I suppose."

"Do be serious, Pamela! Why is it that you can't make up your mind?"

"I don't know. You see, Roddy, you're asking me a very big thing. To many a girl it might possibly be a matter of moments only before she came to a decision, but for me. . . ." She paused, "it's rather different."

"You mean your father?"

She nodded. "Yes! He's all I've got and I'm all he's got. For a father and daughter we are what I suppose Blacon would call a loving couple."

"Do I take it then that you intend to sacrifice yourself on the parental altar?"

"You can put it that way if you like," she answered him seriously. "But honestly, Roddy, there's more to it than just that. I'm not sure of myself. You see, I like you—like you very much—but I don't know whether I love you."

"Is that so terribly important these days?" And again she thought she noticed that same cynicism.

"For you, perhaps not; but for me it's rather important."

"Of course, if you're so utterly old-fashioned about it. . . ."

"I'm not being old-fashioned," she countered. "I'm just being myself. I know that lots of women these days marry for the sheer glamour of it. They crave for new experiences, new sensations. I'm not like that. You may call me pre-Victorian if you like —all lace and lavender—but I do believe that mutual love should play a rather important *rôle* in the drama of marriage, and as I've just told you, I'm not sure that I love you in quite the right way."

Rodney Delisle looked at the girl with a puzzled frown and told himself that he must walk warily. He was quite well aware that village gossip was already linking their names; in fact, he had unobtrusively fanned its flames whenever a suitable opportunity presented itself. What was more, he had no intention of being thwarted by feminine philosophy: Come what may, he was determined to marry Pamela Vance. She was essential to his happiness.

"I suppose our mutual friend Grenville doesn't enter into this discussion?" he asked with a bland smile.

"Why should he?" demanded Pamela. "It's true I like Ian—I like him very much—and if I did marry you, Roddy, that would not prevent my liking him equally as I do at this moment."

"So you're modern enough for that," commented the man with a smile.

"Now you're being hateful," she flashed back at him. "Hadn't we better be getting back before one or the other of us says something which we might regret?"

Delisle was suitably chastened. "There's plenty of time," he placated, "and what's more, if I've inadvertently said something which may have given you offence, I'm sorry."

Pamela was laughing. "Don't be silly, Roddy. It would take more than a mention of Ian to do that. But you must admit he's a nice boy," she followed on swiftly. "There's something so refreshingly naïve about him."

"Something virginal, like the soil," he quoted silkily. "Yes, I'm in agreement with you. Ian's a jolly good fellow. I sometimes wish I were half as good as he. But I can't ever hope for that. I suppose it's because I've had more opportunities for temptation and I've never felt quite comfortable with the Devil behind me."

"If this is the first chapter of the story of your life's indiscretions, Roddy, I think we really *had* better be going. Daddy simply hates my staying out all night."

"Just as you like, Pamela, but I do wish you would give me just a crumb of encouragement."

"It isn't crumbs you want, Roddy," Pamela laughed. "It's the whole cake—and the icing!"

They both laughed, but Delisle was telling himself that she might have chosen a less devastating example!

CHAPTER FIVE

THE DAGGER

SMITH STREET IS one of those criss-cross thoroughfares to the immediate north of Fenchurch Street; a narrow gully of a street with tall, black-façaded buildings.

Bamber Buildings was inscribed in long-faded gilt over the steeply-arched doorway. Inside the building the office cleaners were beginning to congregate with buckets and mops, and it was their habit to begin at the fifth floor and work studiously downwards. They were due to begin operations at six o'clock and, provided that the occupants of the offices had not been abnormally untidy or the day uninvitingly wet, it was reckoned by the caretaker of the block, who was domiciled in a cubicle under the slated roof, that by seven-thirty the last of them would be clear of the premises, dispersing he knew not where.

John Vance knew Smith Street tolerably well. He was equally well-informed of the situation of the offices of Mr. Martin Stone on the second floor. It was dark by the time he arrived. The entrance hall to Bamber Buildings was as gloomy as a mausoleum. On the first landing where the stairway turned to the left a solitary gas-jet flickered from its angled bracket on the wall, for the electrical contractors who had modernised the illumination on behalf of the regal owner of the property had not considered it to be anybody's business to be perambulating the staircase of Bamber Buildings after dark. To this end they had confined the electrical equipment to the actual offices themselves.

A similar jet of light, but one which flickered less, since it was further removed from the main doorway to the building, enabled him to see the name of Martin Stone embossed in white enamelled letters on the black glass panelling of the door.

The man had been calm enough during his journey to London. He had been calm during his leisurely perambulations through the centre of the city towards his destination; but now as he stood before the door of Martin Stone's office he became possessed of an unaccountable nervous tension. The closest analogy he could think of was that of a visit to a dentist and being kept waiting in the ante-room, a prey to fear.

Why he should have felt fearful he could not even guess. Perhaps it was the uncertainty of his mission. If only Stone had even vaguely hinted at the reason for his request that he should call he might not have been standing as he now was with one trembling hand on the outer knob of that door.

He had interviewed many men in his time; some of them in queerer places than this, yet never had he felt the same as he did now. It was altogether inexplicable. It was also very foolish.

Slowly he turned the handle and opened the door. The little outer office with the small square window inscribed "INQUIRIES" was immediately in front of him. An electric pendant hung beyond the wood and glass partition. Vance knocked on the panel, not seeing the white-knobbed electric bell-push on the small shelf-like projection. There was no answer, and he did not knock a second time. He was calmer. His nerves felt pleasantly taut. To the right of him was a door leading into the office beyond. He took a step towards it and pushed it open. Beyond that again and immediately between two desks, one for a typist, whose machine was cloaked with a dust-cover, and the other for a clerk, was another door. It was the door of Stone's office. He was well aware of that. It was an ordinary-looking door with the word "PRIVATE" in black letters on a frosted ground. There was a light in the room beyond. He could see the vague reflection of it through the glass—a more powerful lamp than the one suspended in the outer office. He knocked on the panel with his gloved knuckles.

The only answer he received was silence.

For a full minute he stood there, mute as the wall itself.

Then he knocked again—louder.

Whether it was a trick of his imagination Vance never knew but he thought he heard someone say: "Come in!" Moving to obey, he opened the door with slow precision, watching the room beyond come panoramically into view.

Immediately in front of him was Martin Stone's flat-topped desk. Martin Stone was there, too, but it was not the Martin Stone he had come to see, for the Martin Stone there before him was thrust forward across the desk with something white protruding from between his shoulder-blades.

Martin Stone was dead!

It had always been said in the City that John Vance was a man who made decisions swiftly; that he had never been known to dally with one for more than a minute or two, but under the present circumstances John Vance remained gazing at the terrible sight in front of him for what seemed an interminable stretch of time. It was as though all power of movement had deserted him. Animation was in complete suspension.

Slowly the horror of it faded—filmlike—from his brain. He felt the blood, chill though it was, throbbing in his wrists and temples. He moved forward a step, gazing horror-stricken at the man lying dead. Yet it was not so much the sight of death that caused the panic to leap into his being but the sight of the weapon by which Martin Stone had come by his death. Only the haft of the dagger was visible—a haft carved from the rarest ivory.

Then realisation flooded in on him in a tumultuous cataract that swept him mentally from his feet.

The weapon which had stabbed the life from Martin Stone was his own—one belonging to his own unique collection at Blacon Grange!

It did not seem possible. It was incredible . . . and yet . . . there it was for all to see . . . indisputable proof that he . . . he, John Vance, had murdered Martin Stone.

Serious psychologists tell us that there are emotional crises in the lives of human beings during which the instinct of self-preservation is the dominant one. It is in some way akin to the complex, familiar to the alienist, which expresses itself in the unexplained obsession that the subject stands alone against the hate and conspiracy of his fellows. This phobia imparts to the subject a cunning which, under normal mental states, would be utterly alien to his nature. It is nothing more than the primeval animal in man asserting itself through the ages on his civilising. In a moment of time all the gradations of biological evolution are swept away and the subject becomes once again the animal roaming the forests, fearful that a more powerful animal than himself is lurking in the blue-black shadows, ready with fang and claw to rend him.

The metamorphosis of John Vance was complete. From that terrible moment of realisation he felt that he was no longer a free agent. It was to be his wits against the devices of many. They would hunt him just as primeval man was hunted by the more powerful animals of the teeming forests. The mental crisis had produced a strange man in the trembling shell of himself. From now on it was

John Vance against Power, and in that moment John Vance's instinct of self-preservation became incredibly strong.

Slowly and with the stealth of a beast of prey he crept forward to where the Thing lay across the shining top of the desk. With almost mechanical precision his arm moved out across the intervening space, the fingers wide until, with a gloved caress, they closed upon the carved handle of the dagger. For a moment—but for a moment only—they remained immobile. That one touch of solidarity had irrevocably broken the last strand in his mind that the picture of this room and its horror was a dream, an hallucination; the phantasmagoria of a disordered and diseased mind.

The gloved hand moved upwards and outwards pulling the weapon with it. The blood on the once-gleaming blade sickened him; revolted him; yet curiously enough there was no pity in his heart for the inert Thing whose blood dripped from the still-suspended blade.

Carefully he searched his pockets for handkerchief. Tenderly he wrapped the dagger in its white folds and placed it in the wide pocket of his overcoat. No one must ever know that John Vance's dagger had done this thing. No one must ever know that he had been to Martin Stone's office this night.

With a last look, a look that was almost one of calm disinterest, John Vance turned from the room and switched off the light and followed a similar procedure in the small outer office.

It was only when he was out on the stone landing once more that he appeared to realise that the cold fingers of panic were clutching impatiently at his heart. He turned swiftly and ran blindly down the stairs and out into the light-punctuated street.

Once out of Smith Street, he slackened his pace and walked unhurriedly along Fenchurch Street. Somewhere a clock struck a single chime. Mechanically he looked at his watch. It was seven-fifteen.

As he moved westwards his swinging hand caught against something hard and bulky in his left-hand overcoat pocket. A sickening chill shot through him and he withdrew his hand instantly. A faintness seemed to be creeping across his brain like a delicately indistinct cloud. On the other side of the road he saw the winking lights of a saloon bar.

A moment later he was gulping at a double brandy without soda.

CHAPTER SIX

THE HIDING PLACE

TWIN RIBBONS OF intensely white light danced phantom-like along the dark, twisty road as the Daimler, with John Vance at the wheel, purred effortlessly along between Gloucester and Blacon.

Vance liked driving and particularly driving by night. The headlights' beam sweeping around mysterious dark bends, throwing up the baring hedgerows into fine black and white relief, fascinated him beyond measure. He was not a fast driver. He liked to saunter, and the car was always a willing vehicle.

It was fortunate, he told himself, that he had garaged the car at Gloucester and at a garage whose proprietor was a man of discretion. He had already hinted to the man—Samuel Snape by name—that so far as he was concerned, John Vance had called for the car between six and seven-o'clock in the evening and not at fifteen minutes past eleven. Samuel Snape, knowing a good customer when he met one, had been particularly deferential about it. Of course he understood. Anything that Mr. Vance said was quite good enough for him, and as there had been no mechanic in the garage all day but himself, the favour required little manipulating.

John Vance did not remember quite how long he had remained gulping neat brandy in that London tavern. He did know that he felt wonderfully better as a result of it, and he felt remarkably calm as he took a taxi-cab to the railway station and caught the train for Gloucester.

During the journey he had had plenty of time for thought. He realised the awkwardness of his position. He saw now what a fool he had been to allow Pamela to mention the matter of that letter to anyone. Delisle, of course, would understand how utterly absurd it was that he should desire the death of Stone. In any event, he decided that he had removed his car from that garage in Gloucester between six and seven in the evening and had been amusing himself for a few hours pottering about the countryside in the dark.

31

As the road twisted sharply to the left he slowed down the car's pace to a crawl. He was painfully conscious that such a story sounded ridiculously threadbare. Who would believe that any man would spend his time in such an absurd occupation—driving about for no apparent reason. Vance shivered slightly as he realised the possibility of his being drawn into the affair, but a few miles further along, he consoled himself with the thought that he did not quite see how that was possible. Not a soul knew of his visit that night to London—not even Pamela. The proprietor of the garage in Gloucester would keep his lips closed. He was not in a particularly big way of business, and Vance had that night made a point of overpaying the fellow. If the police discovered any connection between himself and the crime in Stone's office he would take off his hat to them. They would be far cleverer than he thought. He was convinced that no one could possibly know. He smiled to himself. It was a long stretch from London to Gloucester, and when the news came of Stone's death was it not reasonable to assume that the writer of the mysterious letter of a morning or two ago would be satisfied that Vance had carried out his instructions—that he had been faithful to the vow and the last trace of that society would have disappeared?

To Vance, nearing Blacon, the situation was watertight. But then John Vance had had a terrific shock, and he had consumed so much brandy that his brain had not the swift clarity of argument that it normally possessed. Moreover, John Vance, despite his success in the City, imagined that he could persuade others with the same facility with which he could persuade himself—a bad fault in a man fighting the law. Nevertheless, he assured himself, he had thought himself into a more stable frame of mind than that of a few hours ago when he had withdrawn the dagger from the shoulders of the dead stockbroker. That had been a nightmare he would not readily forget.

He drove up the drive of Blacon Grange and round to the garage. Having stabled the car, he walked leisurely to the front of the house. He felt singularly confident, despite the fact that the ominous bulge in the pocket of his overcoat reminded him of the events of the past few hours.

Birtles met him in the spacious hall.

"Miss Pamela is in the lounge, sir."

"Is she alone, Birtles?"

"No, sir. Mr. Delisle is with her."

"What time is it, Birtles?" asked Vance, casually enough.

The butler looked at his watch. "Eleven forty-two, sir."

"Really, as late as all that! Why, Birtles, I must have been driving around the Gloucestershire lanes for nearly three hours! Still, it's a beautiful night, Birtles; one of those nights that brings out all the latent poetry in a man's soul. Have you ever felt that you had hidden within you a poetic soul?"

Birtles was too well trained to look surprised at this questioning.

"Not that I can recall, sir," he answered in his unruffled tones. "Poetry is scarcely in my line. Shall I take your coat, sir?"

Vance started and ceased instantly to unbutton the garment.

"No—that is to say, Birtles, I've just remembered, that Miss Pamela wanted to sew the lining of one of the sleeves. She was telling me of it yesterday—scolding me a little, I might say. If I don't remind her about it, she will be annoyed."

"Very good, sir. Will you have some whisky?"

"Good idea, Birtles. The nights are growing chilly. Poetry doesn't keep out the cold!"

Vance crossed the hall and watched the butler vanish through the small, oak-panelled door to the left of the staircase. As soon as the door had closed, John Vance ran lightly up the stairs to his room. Switching on the light, he pulled from his pocket the blood-stained handkerchief containing a dagger which had sent Martin Stone to eternity. For a moment the old horror and fear swept down upon him in a torrent. The events of the night crowded in on him in a suffocating press. Swiftly he opened the door of the tall wardrobe and dropped the bundle on to the floor. Locking the door, he placed the key in his pocket, and taking off his coat he threw it over a chair. Then he went downstairs to Pamela.

"Daddy!" exclaimed the girl as he opened the door of the lounge. "Wherever have you been? Do you realise that it's nearly midnight?"

"Just pottering around," he answered, dropping leisurely into a chair in front of the fire. "I went over to Gloucester this afternoon in the car. I left it at a garage and decided that walking would be good for my health. I walked over the hills to Micheldean and back again by road. It was between six and seven o'clock when I got to the garage, and as the night looked so attractive I just drove around the lanes for an hour or two. As nearly as I can remember," he smiled, "I spent the time in the contemplation of the beauties of the firmament and thinking about life in general."

"And you've had no food—nothing since lunchtime?" Pamela, woman-like, took the obvious practical viewpoint.

"Not hungry," he said laconically. "I've sent Birtles for a drink," he added. "You'd better have one, too, Delisle."

"Thank you," responded the young man with a smile.

Just then Birtles entered with the tray and dispensed the spirit with a ritual which the butler had perfected over an experience of many years.

Pamela seated herself on the arm of her father's chair. She was worried. It was unlike him to wander about all by himself in the car. There was something on his mind, and she had a good idea what that something was. In the brief silence that followed came the sound of the telephone bell ringing out in the hall. Pamela was certain that her father started at the sound. A moment later Birtles returned.

"Someone asking for Mr. Delisle," he announced.

Delisle excused himself and went out of the room.

When he had gone, Pamela turned to her father: "You're still not worrying about that silly letter?" she asked.

"Of course not! Why, I've scarcely given the wretched thing a thought all day!"

"I'm so glad, Daddy, but I couldn't help thinking it was so unlike you to drive about at night all by yourself."

Vance smiled up at her and patted her hand affectionately. "Must we always be the slaves of routine?" he asked, smiling a little wryly. "I do wish you wouldn't worry so much about me. I'm quite all right," he added simply.

Delisle returned, bland and smiling.

"So sorry that people should be 'phoning around to find me like this, but I've been expecting a call all the evening, and I gave your number just in case I didn't happen to have returned home."

"My dear boy, don't worry about that. I know what it's like to be hunted about on the telephone," laughed Vance.

"Well, I'm afraid I'll have to be pushing off," announced the young man. "See you tomorrow, Pamela, I hope," he smiled as he held out his hand.

"I'll be out for a gallop at the usual time, I expect," she told him.

"Good-night, sir, and—thank you."

Delisle grasped Vance's hand and held it for a moment and the eyes of the two men met.

"Good-night," responded Vance, "and thank for looking after Pamela."

~ ~ ~ ~ ~

Pamela lay in her bed thinking; she was not yet certain in her own mind that her father had ban speaking the truth when he had told her that he had given no further thought to the matter of the mysterious letter. There was something about him tonight that was not altogether natural. She knew his every mood intimately. If he thought to deceive her, he did not know daughter as well as he pretended to do. All that talk about admiring the beauties of nocturnal nature! She almost laughed into the darkness about her as the recollection of his explanation came to her. Her father had never been a man to grow lyrical about sunsets and mountains and the moonlight on the heather. That wasn't his nature. He was more practical, and any affection in his make-up had always been reserved for herself.

Thinking of these things, she fell asleep.

In his room, John Vance did not go immediately to bed. He had work to do—work of considerable importance. He must get rid of that Thing that lay at the bottom of his wardrobe. So far he had borne the strain remarkably well, but he felt that he had done so at the expense of his bottled-up emotions. Now that strain was beginning to tell. He had asked Birtles to leave him a decanter and a glass on a tray beside his bed on the excuse that he felt he had a "cold coming on."

It was many more minutes before he could steel himself to unlock the door of the wardrobe and bring out that bundle of damnably incriminating evidence. Where could he hide it? Where could he hide it where it would never be found? Slowly he unwrapped the dark-stained handkerchief from around the dagger. There it lay in the folds. He did not touch it . . . just looked at it with a feeling of reverence. There was nothing revolting about it. He seemed to be able to divorce its sinister significance from his love of it. For he did love it—loved all his collection of old weapons which he had acquired from odd corners of the globe over a long period of years.

As he looked at it a thought came into his mind that made him wonder why it had been absent so long. How was it that this small dagger from his collection had got into the hands of Martin Stone's assassin? How was it he had never missed it from his collection—from its accustomed place in the long oaken rack where all the others had reposed?

This was a problem that might exercise his imagination and perhaps his investigations in the future. But not just yet, he warned himself. No, certainly not just yet!

With a gesture of helplessness he looked around the room for a suitable and safe hiding place. At other moments he felt that a dozen

or more likely places would immediately have occurred to him.
Where did people hide things they desperately wanted to be rid
of . . . people in novels? He had never been a particularly great
reader. He had never had much time for that in a busy, money-
making life, but he recalled to mind that he had once read of
someone hiding money under a loose board in the floor and relaying
the carpet on the top of it. Vance turned back the Persian carpet and
gazed thoughtfully at the sombre black floor-boards. Age had
warped some of them slightly. He pressed them apprehensively
with his nervous fingers. They were all very secure.

Dejectedly he replaced the carpet into position and looked once
again around the room. Then his eyes lingered on the little bureau
standing over there in the corner. It was years since he had last used
that bureau. Year ago, when had been more actively engaged in
business, he had sometimes awakened in the middle of the night
remembering some important business and, lest he should forget
before the morning, he had been in the habit of throwing on his
dressing-gown and making an immediate note of it seated at his
bureau. On the top of the bureau stood a desk calendar—one of
those stoutly-built wooden affairs with the day of the week, the day
of the month and the name of the month all operated by means of
little rollers, the knobs projecting on the sides for the purpose of
winding.

Suddenly, as he contemplated it, he recalled that the back of the
calendar was made in the form of a slide running in narrow grooves,
so that the mechanism, simple though it was, was easily available in
the event of any of the rollers becoming jammed. Mentally he
measured the height of the calendar. It was about nine inches in
height. The length of the straight-bladed dagger on the floor at his
feet was not more than eight inches overall.

Crossing to the closed bureau, he lifted down the calendar and
slid out the back panel. The aperture revealed a cavity of just sufficient depth, he calculated, to contain the weapon and the handkerchief.

Tremblingly he replaced the corners of the square of linen across
the weapon without touching it with his naked fingers. Then he
proceeded to wrap it more tightly in its blood-soaked shroud and
placed it within the cavity. Then he twirled the roller-knobs at the
side and found that they were unobstructed. Finally he replaced the
slide and stood the calendar back again on the bureau.

John Vance heaved a sigh of relief and began to prepare for bed.

~ ~ ~ ~ ~

Next morning Pamela was awakened by the maid knocking on the panel of the door.

The maid entered and, as was her custom, placed a silver tray containing the girl's morning tea and a folded copy of that morning's newspaper on the table beside the bed. Then she crossed the room and drew back the curtains.

"Thank you, Marie," smiled Pamela, sleepily. "Any thrilling news this morning?"

"Why, yes, miss. There's been another murder in London—gentleman stabbed to death in his office chair. Horrible, I think it is."

A sudden spasm of fear clutched the girl's heart. She felt the blood drain from her face.

"Thank you, Marie," she repeated mechanically, "I don't think I shall trouble to read about that."

But no sooner had the girl left the room than Pamela snatched the newspaper from the table and opened it. A black, ominous headline told her of the death of a well-known stockbroker. The print became blurred as she read of the murder of Martin Stone while seated at his desk in his city office the night before.

For a moment she felt stunned. The man her father had been instructed to murder *had* been murdered.

Throwing on her dressing-gown, she raced across the landing to her father's room and flung wide the door. He was still asleep. She shook him wildly by the shoulder. "Daddy! Daddy!" she cried chokingly. "Martin Stone has been murdered—d'you hear me? . . . *Murdered!*"

CHAPTER SEVEN

INSPECTOR BURKE

CHIEF INSPECTOR CURTIS Burke sat at his desk at Scotland Yard humming the refrain from a popular radio dance tune.

To the uninitiated it might have appeared as if Mr. Burke was in a somewhat happy, care-free frame of mind. On the contrary, he was in the throes of a particularly nasty little problem.

The musical obligato was entirely extraneous to the problem, and in this respect he most nearly resembled his late chief, Superintendent Whatmoth, whose repertoire of tunes suitable for humming was considered the most comprehensive in the force, but who was always known to be nearing the end of his difficulties when the depressing tempo of "The Dead March" was heard issuing from between his loosely held lips.

Curtis Burke was not like old Whatmoth. At the age of thirty he had achieved considerable success in his chosen profession, which consisted in turning his hand to anything in the line of crime from the delinquencies of night club "queens" to the activities of the banditry of Soho. He had come to Scotland Yard via Cambridge, where he had been considered a good student in a rather more general than in any specialised department. From the uniformed branch he had quickly graduated to the indoor staff, and now he was a chief inspector—a title he had well earned as a result of his proficiency in most of the branches of crime detection to which he brought a brain sharpened by considerable analytical study.

In appearance he was spare and athletic—the holder of the mile record on the track. His hair was dark and inclined to be wavy, the envy of two sisters living in Warwickshire, whose hair, it will be gathered, required the frequent ministrations of an expert in that branch of beauty's art. His eyes were blue, a relic most probably from his remote Irish ancestry, who were recorded as having a reputation for restlessness somewhere around Donegal.

Mr. Burke—which was how the majority of his colleagues addressed him—had not been to bed all that night and it was now nine o'clock in the morning. He had, in fact, been paying considerable attention to the affair in Smith Street, where a certain Martin Stone, stockbroker, had been discovered by an office cleaner dead in his chair at his desk. Further scrutiny on the part of Constable Travis, who had been summoned to the building in order to reassure Mrs. Ellen Withers, the cleaner in question, that the evidence of her own eyes was eminently reliable, had elicited the fact that the man had been stabbed between the shoulder-blades at the back of the heart, and further than that, the weapon was to be found nowhere in the room.

Burke—which was the name by which his superiors nearly always addressed him—had been set a pretty problem—as pretty a problem, in fact, as it was possible for the most academic of the mystery novelists to invent. Here was a man dead in his office chair with not the smallest clue, as yet, to the identity of the murderer or the reason for this sudden despatch of an apparently respectable and highly-thought-of member of the business community to those regions which, despite investigation, are as yet uncharted.

Almost as soon as the crime had been discovered Burke had been summoned and had taken automatic charge of the case. Constable Travis had contributed his statement, likewise had Mrs. Ellen Withers, the office cleaner who, at ten minutes past seven, had switched on the light in Stone's private office and had "discovered" the crime. The routine work had followed swiftly. Doctor Northop, the divisional surgeon, had made his examination and report; the photographers had exposed a number of plates; the fingerprint men had been dusting for an hour, working inch by inch around the room, and finally the body had been removed.

Burke until now had paid scant attention to this side of the case. That was not his job. It was his task to find the person who had struck Martin Stone down. To assist him to this desirable end he had made a number of notes on a sheet of foolscap; he had taken immediate charge of the unemptied wastepaper basket in the knee-hole of the man's desk; he had sealed the safe and likewise the drawers of the desk and the filing cabinet. Constable Travis could not for the life of him understand the inspector's object in this routine, considering he had been detailed to remain on duty inside the office until relieved next morning. But Burke believed in thoroughness. He didn't want anything removed—however inadvertently—from that office until he had submitted everything to a detailed examination.

Another report on the desk in front of him was from Sergeant Pace, who, armed with a list of names and addresses of Martin Stone's office staff, had visited each and all of them in their respective homes and taken statements from them. The staffs of other offices on the same floor had been equally surprised to receive a nocturnal visit from another Scotland Yard officer who demanded answers to a number of questions. It was the first cast of the net.

The second cast was more difficult, but it was now in progress. It consisted in tracing every caller to the office of Martin Stone, not only on the day of the crime, but on several days immediately preceding. Then would come the equally difficult task of checking up on Martin Stone's own activities during the week, and later a much more detailed tunnelling into his past life.

This much Burke had already learned. Martin Stone was a bachelor. His age was fifty. He had been in business in the City for fifteen years. Before coming to London he had been in Manchester, and twenty years ago it was said that he had been in America, and also that he was not altogether unknown in Mexico.

All these details Burke had pencilled on his sheet of foolscap. On a separate sheet he had his own diagram of the office; the position of the desk, and also a sketch of the body. Next came a list of the contents oi the dead man's pockets. His wallet had contained ten pounds in treasury notes; a pocket case; a number of letters of a private nature and seven business cards. The loose change in the hip pocket amounted to six shillings and fivepence halfpenny.

Martin Stone lived in Crouch End in a small detached house. He had a housekeeper, Mrs. Simms, who lived on the premises with her son, John, who was a porter at Covent Garden. Burke had just returned to the Yard from interviewing Mrs. Simms. She had been able to tell him very little. Mr. Stone, he gathered, was a quiet, unobtrusive man. He had left home yesterday morning at his usual time, which was nine-thirty. She had expected him home as usual at seven-thirty for his dinner, but at five o'clock he had telephoned to say that he might be a little later—eight o'clock to eight-thirty. He had not told her the reason for this delay, but Mrs. Simms had assumed that it was due to business affairs. Burke had left the house with the strict injunction that she must admit no one until she heard from him again.

On the surface the crime appeared meaningless and motiveless, but Burke had not the slightest intention of deluding himself on that score.

Had there been a motive "sticking out," as he phrased it, he would have been even more suspicious. Doctor Northop had given it as his opinion that the weapon used for the committal of the crime had been a bladed one—either a knife or a short dagger. The doctor had gone to considerable lengths to explain to the inspector the difference in appearance of wounds caused through the use of different types of instruments. Burke had listened courteously but without interest. All he cared about was that he had to look out for a weapon answering to the medical man's vague yet precise description—a task more difficult than looking for the proverbial needle.

Burke looked at the clock and saw that it was nine-fifteen. Then he remembered that he had neither breakfasted nor shaved, and since there was not time to go to his home for the purpose, he put on his hat and coat and went out.

Three-quarters of an hour later he was back again in his room. Sergeant Pace was waiting for him, and with the officer was a small, narrow-chested whippet of a man named Rodgers, who said he was Martin Stone's clerk.

"Sit down, Mr. Rodgers," invited Burke easily. "I want you to answer a few questions. There's not the slightest need for you to be nervous, even if this is the first time you've been down to Scotland Yard. I can tell you—confidentially—that you are not under suspicion."

Mr. Rodgers smiled and blinked at Burke from behind the windows of his horn-rimmed spectacles.

"What is it you wish to know?" he asked in a thin, half-apologetic voice.

"Well," Burke began, "you can tell us what sort of business you dealt in."

"Quite a general business," he replied. "In these days a stockbroker can't afford to pick and choose. Any kind of share business at all. I can show you the books if you wish, sir."

"That will come later, Mr. Rodgers. What I mean is, was the business 'on the square' as they call it, or was it . . . well, Mr. Rodgers, you know what I'm getting at, I'm sure." Burke's smile was disarming, and in the case of a man such as Mr. Rodgers it was essential that it should have been.

Burke noticed that the man hesitated, but it was only for a moment. He was wise enough to realise that to prevaricate in that building would do him no good at all.

"Well, sir," he began, "I suppose there can be few firms such as ours possessed of an entirely unblemished reputation. Mr. Stone was a business man. He was not in the habit of turning down business just because it might be a matter of conscience. I can recall one or two deals that were not strictly what you would say 'above board.' Is that what you wish to know, sir?"

"Partly," said Burke, "but I'm afraid I'm an inquisitive fellow, Mr. Rodgers. You've whetted my appetite. Now, do you think you could remember any details of those particular transactions?"

Mr. Rodgers appeared thoughtful for a moment, although Burke felt that the fellow had the details on the tip of his tongue if he cared to admit it.

"There was a scheme about three years ago relating to oil in Mexico. I didn't like it, sir. I was presumptuous enough to mention to Mr. Stone that I didn't like it either, and if I remember correctly he told me he thought I must be growing old."

"By which he meant that old men sometimes regain their consciences," interjected the detective. "I understand, Mr. Rodgers. More than that, I sympathise with you."

Mr. Rodgers expanded somewhat under the subtle blandishment.

"Of course, sir, I'm not saying that the scheme might not have turned up trumps, because Mr. Stone knew the Mexican market remarkably well. I believe he'd once been out there . . . many years before he opened up in London."

"And how did the venture progress?"

"It didn't, sir. Thousands of people lost tidy sums," was the surprising reply.

Burke appeared unaffected by the answer.

"How much would that be?"

"Altogether about twenty thousand pounds."

"Was the company floated in London?" Burke was growing interested.

"No, sir. In New York. Mr. Stone was the London broker and worked the prospectus on the Stock Market here."

Burke looked thoughtful and added a few more lines to his notes.

"I may want to see you again about this, Mr. Rodgers," he smiled, rising from his chair and holding out his hand. "Good morning! I take it we can always find you at your home address?"

"For the present, sir, you most certainly can," replied Mr. Rodgers ruefully.

CHAPTER EIGHT

BURKE VISITS BLACON

THE INQUEST ON the body of Martin Stone had been opened and adjourned. The newspapers gave the story due prominence and hinted, with their usual audacity, that Scotland Yard were following up a number of likely clues and that it was hoped that the murderer would be duly apprehended.

The affair had already been tagged in Fleet Street as "The Office Murder," and Burke found himself besieged for news of Scotland Yard's activities. Many of these Fleet Street men were decent fellows, and Burke hated to have to tell them that they would have to make their own "stories" of the investigations so far as he was concerned. He would certainly have liked to have given them a few facts, because he knew something of the life they led in Fleet Street. Reporters were expected to write a "story" every day about the murder. None of them could go back to the office and tell the news editor that Scotland Yard was dumb, for if Scotland Yard might be so afflicted, that worthy could always be counted on not to be!

Sorry as Burke was for the plight of the newspaper men, he was even more sorry for himself. He had, for one thing, so little on which to work. It was true that the man Rodgers had given him a glimmer of hope when he had mentioned about the Mexican oil syndicate that had proved a palpable swindle, but even that glimmer was a rather faint one. It was just possible, he argued, that someone who had lost heavily in that oil ramp had been sore about it. And who wouldn't be? It was equally possible that any of these people who had lost sums of varying amounts in that twenty thousand pounds subscription might have so brooded over the loss that they had, in the end, decided that Martin Stone ought to be "bumped off." To Burke's mind that was a quite logical sequel, but to trace that person was going to be much more difficult. It would necessitate a close investigation of the books of the firm, a task which might conceivably involve many weeks of strenuous routine work. Still, it had to be done.

Burke's investigation of Stone's office occupied him for the best part of the morning, and when he had finished a Scotland Yard van had removed everything of interest down to the Yard, where the sifters were immediately put on the job.

For an hour after lunch Burke was reading the reports. There was the police surgeon's. That told him nothing more than he already knew. The fatal blow had been delivered some time between six-fifteen and seven o'clock and that Martin Stone had died almost instantly. The position of the body proved that the assassin had done his work from behind and out of sight of the murdered man. That was the only established fact in the case and, curiously enough, it was to Burke the fact that mattered least of all.

The report of the print men was even more unsatisfactory. The finger-prints in the office had all been accounted for between the staff, the dead man and the office cleaners. There remained now only the dead man's private papers and the record of the firm's transactions.

The detective, feeling that he was getting nowhere, cut with his pocket-knife the string of a brown paper parcel on the desk in front of him. The parcel consisted of a number of pocket diaries he had found in the safe extending over a period of seven years, and also a bundle of letters which had been kept apart from the business correspondence in a drawer in the desk.

He spread the miscellaneous collection out on the desk and began with the letters. One of them caused him to elevate his eyebrows. It was from a woman and signed "Marcelle."

"Marcelle" was a lady who obviously knew what she wanted, and the tone of the letter made that very apparent. She wanted money; nay, she demanded it, and demanded it with a threat. "The matter must no longer be made light of," she had written. "I am in no mood to argue further with you. I will give you seven days to pay me what I have a right to demand."

Burke sighed. How so very like a woman. The letter was undated and contained no address. Death, he reflected, was a great inquisitor. In life it was probable that Martin Stone might have succeeded in concealing this obviously coarse intrigue. In death everything was laid bare—everything, that was, except the essential facts.

Yet the letter was significant. If only "Marcelle" had dated it!

"Just my luck," he murmured, as he reached out for another letter.

Fortunately this one was dated. It was dated February 17th, 1933, but like the other it bore no address. He read it with increasing interest. Reference was made to the "Mexican Oil Scandal," and the writer, who signed himself "A Victim," mentioned that he wished he had taken the advice of John Vance, who had warned him against having anything to do with the scheme. "I did not trust John Vance, but now I wish I had done so," complained Mr. Anonymous.

Burke pursed his lips as he looked at the single sheet of note-paper.

Now, who the devil was John Vance? Burke felt that the name was familiar to him, but try as he might he could not place it. He telephoned to "Inquiries" and asked for information, which was forthcoming in an incredibly short space of time. Of course, he remembered now. "Inquiries" must think that the case was turning his brain. John Vance was the stockbroker who had retired a few years ago; reputed to be wealthy. He was now living in Hereford-shire, at Blacon Grange. Burke added John Vance's name to his notes. Perhaps later on he would run over and have a word with Vance—Vance might be able to tell him something about this Mexican Oil affair.

The next item that came to his hand was an engagement pad, which he had taken from the dead man's desk. On the line prefaced by October 11th were the pencilled words; "Ring up Vance." That was all, and October 11th was the day before Martin Stone had been murdered. The detective arose slowly from his desk. He felt that his interview with John Vance must be made immediately. He must know what it was that Martin Stone said when he telephoned to Vance—if he had telephoned at all.

Before ringing up to discover whether John Vance was at Bla-con, Burke sent an officer round to see Rodgers, to inquire whether Vance had been among the callers at the office on the fatal day. Then he asked for discreet inquiries to be made of the police at Blacon as to whether Vance was in residence at the Grange. Three-quarters of an hour later Curtis Burke was in the west-bound train with the knowledge that Vance had not called at the office and that he was, at that moment, at Blacon Grange.

~ ~ ~ ~ ~

Ian Grenville had packed up at the farm after a busy day and had strolled around to "The Sickle" to see whether Joe Myercroft, the innkeeper, had any poaching information.

Joe Myercroft was a very useful person to Grenville. Many a time he had overheard some quite valuable poaching gossip in the taproom, and as there had been something of an epidemic of poaching on the estate recently, he wanted to know whether Joe had anything to tell him.

But for once Joe was despondent. Business in the taproom was not what it was. Even on market-days the customers were usually well known to him, and "foreigners" were few and rather far between.

On his way home Grenville had to pass the railway station. The London train was drawing out again as he came up to the level-crossing gates and waited. As the gates opened Grenville's eyes opened wider, for advancing from the platform side was none other than dear old Curtis Burke, whom he hadn't seen more than twice since the old Cambridge days.

Recognition even in the quickly lowering twilight was mutual.

"If it isn't old Curty!" exclaimed Grenville.

"And the same to you, Squire!" greeted the detective. "I suppose you are the squire of these wilds?" he added quickly.

Ian Grenville laughed. "Not yet," he said, "but you never know! But to what are we indebted for this utterly unexpected visit? You can't be on holiday?"

"And why not?" asked Burke. "I'm sure it's very delightful down here."

"Incorrigible as ever," laughed Grenville, taking the detective's arm. "But now you are here we're jolly well going to swap stories. What about a refresher at 'The Sickle'?"

"Excellent speech," enthused Burke. "Lead me to 'The Sickle,' brother. But not for long, mark you. I am on business bent"—this in a whisper—"and I'd like to get the ten-thirty-three back to town."

"You're going to sleep this night at the old homestead or my name's not Grenville," announced he of that name as they marched together into the parlour of "The Sickle."

But Burke shook his head. "It's nice of you, old man, but my business is urgent. Ever heard about an affair the newspapers call 'The Office Murder'?"

Joe Myercroft at that moment punctuated the conversation with a tray containing two pewter pots of nut-brown ale.

"You mean the one where a man was stabbed to death in his office?"

"Just that, my son, and Detective Inspector Burke, of Scotland Yard, has uncoiled one of the law's famous tentacles in your precious little village of Blacon. Can you beat it?"

"I should say not. You know, I'd forgotten for the moment that you were such an important person, Curty. But why Blacon? Really, you know, you ought to stay here at least for a night to understand our peaceful, kindly natures! Are we supposed to be shielding the murderer?"

Curtis Burke shook his head.

"I certainly hope not, for the sake of Blacon's reputation. It really does appear quite unspoiled, doesn't it? By the way, do you know anything of a man named Vance—lives at Blacon Grange, I hear."

Ian Grenville nearly choked as he quickly set down his pot on the table.

"You don't mean to say that Vance has anything to do with the murder, do you?"

"You go a yard too fast for me, old man," smiled Burke. "I don't recollect saying anything of the sort. I asked you whether you knew him."

"Know him? Good lord, yes," laughed Grenville. "And his daughter Pamela. We're quite good friends."

"So," commented Burke darkly, "that's how things are in the Hundred of Blacon, eh? Young squire and wealthy man's daughter. Pretty country romance. Wedding bells for village belle! Don't tell me it's not true. Remember, I'm a detective, and when a young man blushes when he mentions a girl by name the Book of Deduction says 'Guilty.' "

"You've been reading the headlines of the Yankee papers," laughed Grenville. "As a matter of fact I wish what you have suggested was true. It isn't. She's a ripping girl, though. You wait until you've seen her . . . and her father, charming fellow."

Grenville called for Joe's ministrations a second time.

"Do I understand that the daughter oi the wealthy man does not honour young squire with her favours? Tut-tut, my son! Your inferiority complex does you little credit!"

"It isn't that . . ." began Grenville, and paused, uncertain how he ought to proceed.

"Once again the Book of Deductions says 'There is a rival.' Isn't that so?"

Grenville nodded.

"Right again! Yes, there is—a regular bounder of a fellow. Name of Delisle. Can't stand him at any price. He's got a little place on the other side of the hill. What Pamela sees in him I can never understand. Aren't women queer? Fall for such obvious blighters, I mean."

"Here's to the downfall of the rival," said Burke seriously, raising his tankard to his lips. "You've sure got it badly, old man. Wish I could stay a week or two to see the battle. If I know anything about you, you're not going to give in without a spot of bother."

"I wish it were all as easy as you make it appear with your blarney," Grenville told him; then pushing the subject to one side: "But you haven't told me what connection John Vance has with that murder in London that you're investigating."

"That's just it," said Burke. "I don't know. Probably nothing at all. If Vance is in a reasonable frame of mind he may be able to give me a line on the case. They were both stockbrokers. I came across his name in some papers in Stone's office."

"You came across his name? The papers must have been pretty ancient, because Vance told me himself that he's been right out of the business for years."

"Maybe, but you see I've an idea that Vance may know of someone who particularly wanted Mr. Martin Stone put out of the way. It's strange how sometimes the slenderest chances lead to important clues. We have to follow every thread. How far is it from here to Blacon Grange?" he asked suddenly.

"Not more than fifteen minutes brisk walking. I'll come along with you if you like . . . introduce you and all that. Pamela's sure to be there. You'll like her."

"I'm sure I shall. You always had superb judgment. Ever been to Town on the ten-thirty-three? What sort of a train is it?"

"No, never," confessed Grenville, "but if you miss it, promise me you'll stay up with us. Father will be delighted to meet you again."

"That pleasure would be mutual," smiled Burke, "but I'm afraid it will still have to be deferred. You see, I hate missing trains."

They went out of "The Sickle" arm-in-arm.

But Burke was not to get the ten-thirty-three that night!

CHAPTER NINE

THE MISSING DAGGER

IT WAS QUITE dark by the time the two young men arrived at Blacon Grange, but Burke felt confident that he could trust Grenville to know every inch of the way.

Birtles opened the door to them—the suave, imperturbable Birtles. If the gentlemen would wait he would inquire whether Mr. Vance could see them.

They stood together in the square oak-panelled hall where once cavalier and roundhead had no doubt rolled together. Burke had always been fascinated by old houses. They had an atmosphere that intrigued him. He regarded them as being much more vital pages of history than those he had been prone to find elsewhere.

His companion, he noted, had stepped forward with a gesture of: "Thanks, Birtles—we're quite at home," but the butler had been studiously formal as he bade them wait, and it was patent to Burke that Grenville's stock in the matrimonial market was none too good at the moment.

"I can't understand what's come over Birtles," he heard Grenville protesting, but Burke was not listening with full attention, for on the farther side of the hall, adjacent to the beginning of the wide staircase, there hung an elaborately carved oak rack containing a remarkable assortment of old weapons, from the smallest dagger to the fiercest sabre. Burke stood in front of the collection fascinated. Some of the daggers had jewelled handles; others plain ivory; others, again, just common horn. He counted them methodically. Beginning at the left-hand corner of the rack he counted fifteen, but nevertheless he saw that there should have been sixteen, for one of the tough hide straps through which ran the blades was empty.

Burke attached little importance to the matter. He certainly did not connect it with the murder of Martin Stone. After all, lots of people had dagger collections, and if he were to investigate every collection in the country, the case might last him the remainder of his life.

It was then that the opening of a door broke in on his thoughts. He turned and saw a remarkably pretty girl advancing down on Grenville with an unmistakable smile of friendship on her cherry-red lips.

"Good gracious, Ian," she cried, "I'd no idea you were calling around tonight. Daddy's been busy having a billiards match with Roddy. They're still at it. I've sent Birtles to tell them you're here."

Grenville looked confused. The colour mounted to his cheeks. Burke thought he appeared like a tongue-tied schoolboy having his first conversation with a girl.

"As a matter of fact, I hadn't thought of coming tonight," he told her awkwardly. "I really offered to introduce my old friend, Burke. He's come down from London especially to interview your father, Pamela. Let me introduce Chief Inspector Curtis Burke, of Scotland Yard."

Burke advanced towards the girl smilingly, but he saw that she hesitated. Her face seemed suddenly to have grown paler.

"You really mustn't be frightened of me, Miss Vance," he assured her. "I'm quite harmless. I just wanted to have a quiet chat with your father on a matter of business. You see, it sometimes happens that Scotland Yard has to ask the assistance of all sorts and conditions of people when we are investigating an important case, and as your father may possibly be able to give me some information, here I am. Not intruding, I hope?"

Pamela Vance recovered her poise quickly. She realised that her hesitation, however momentary it may have appeared, had been noticed by the detective.

"I think you are the first real detective I've ever met," Pamela said, laughing. "For the moment Ian's introduction quite took my breath away. I do hope, Mr. Burke, that you didn't think me rude standing here staring at you like that?"

"A charming young lady can never be guilty of rudeness." Burke handed out the compliment gallantly. "Did I hear you say that your father could spare me a few moments?"

But before she could reply John Vance came towards them from the direction of the billiards room. He nodded genially to Ian and turned to Burke.

"You are Mr. Burke? Birtles tells me you are from Scotland Yard and that you want to have a chat with me?" John Vance's voice was level and icily calm.

"That is so, Mr. Vance. I was lucky enough to find my old friend Grenville down in Blacon village and he kindly offered to bring me up here and introduce me."

"Yes, that's right," put in Grenville. "Burke's one of the cleverest men at the Yard and he's working on that London murder case. You remember, sir, a man was murdered in his office a day or two ago?"

"Of course," nodded Vance. "I remember the case. Pamela was expressing herself in no uncertain tones on the subject, weren't you, Pamela? But come this way, Mr. Burke, we'll go into the library; there's a fire there."

The two men crossed the hall together.

"Mayn't I come, too?" asked Pamela in a disappointed voice. "I've never heard anyone being put through third degree methods."

"I should hate to disappoint you, young lady," smiled Burke, over his shoulder, "but there won't be anything like that. If you want my advice you'll have a nice little talk with Grenville. But I warn you, Miss Vance, you must not pay too much attention to anything he may say about myself. The country air has played havoc with his imagination. . . ."

Inside the library John Vance indicated a chair, rang for Birtles and ordered whisky.

"Now, Mr. Burke," he began, briskly business-like, "what is it I can do for you?"

Burke outlined the case to the ex-financier and mentioned the little details that had made him make a hurried journey to Blacon.

"Do you think you could give me any information at all about this Mexican oil business?" he asked in conclusion.

"Will you take soda or water with your drink, Mr. Burke?" asked Vance, as he poured out the spirit, and Burke signified his preference for water.

"I'm afraid I can tell you very little you do not already know," began Vance. "I remember the swindle perfectly, and I was frankly surprised that Stone had anything at all to do with it. On reflection, I was charitable enough to assume that Stone—who was well known to me in the course of my business associations in London—like most other brokers, firmly believed in the authenticity of the flotation. I have known many stockbrokers, Mr. Burke, who have from time to time expressed the utmost and implicit confidence in certain ventures entirely on the strength of some influential person's association with them, even though their better judgments should have warned them against such things.

"Now you have mentioned it, I remember that at the time when subscriptions were taken up—and the prospectus, mark you, was thoroughly attractive—I received a number of letters from old clients asking my advice, and in each and every case I recommended that they should not touch the issue under any circumstances."

"What reasons had you, Mr. Vance, for forming such an opinion?" Burke was by now genuinely interested in the man.

Vance replied with a touch of bitterness: "I have seen too many swindles worked over oil ramps in Mexico, Mr. Burke, and you may take it from me that if the affair had been a genuine one plenty of perfectly good money could have been found in America without troubling to put it on the London market."

"That sounds common sense to me," Burke admitted. "I suppose you haven't a list of the people who wrote you at that time?"

John Vance smiled as he shook his head.

"It must be quite three years ago. I doubt if I could so much as recall a single name."

Burke was disappointed—felt as if his journey down to Blacon had been so much wasted time.

"Do you happen to have such a thing as a list of your old clients?" he asked desperately.

"I might possibly be able to let you have that," Vance agreed slowly, "but I'm afraid it would have to be compiled entirely from memory. You see, Mr. Burke, I've been out of active participation in business for a number of years and all my books have been destroyed."

"If you could manage to think back for me I shall be eternally grateful," confessed the detective.

"Tell me, Mr. Burke," pursued Vance, "do you suspect that the murderer was someone who had been ruined as a result of the Mexican oil swindle?"

Burke nodded his head slowly. "That is what I have at the back of my mind, sir. But up to the moment," he added, "it is about the only thing I really have to bite on."

"It is, of course, possible," said Vance, slowly and deliberately, and Burke noted that the elder man's face held a rather thoughtful and determined look, "and if I can do anything at all to help you, Mr. Burke, I shall be only too willing to do so."

Burke was not, however, to know what an intense strain the interview had been for John Vance as they left the room together in search of Pamela and Grenville. It had been the sternest struggle in self-control Vance ever remembered, and he felt, too, that had

Burke come to Blacon to question him on matters other than he had done, it was just possible that the detective would have held an altogether different opinion of him.

"Are you returning to London tonight?" asked Vance as he opened the door leading to the lounge on the farther side of the hall.

"That had been my intention." There was a note of doubt in the detective's voice as his eyes sought the collection of weapons on the opposite wall beside the staircase. "But I'm none too sure. I detest travelling in railway trains at night and seldom do so more than I can possibly help."

"I was thinking that if you weren't returning I might offer you hospitality?"

"That's charming of you, Mr. Vance, but if I do stay it will have to be with Grenville. As a matter of fact I've already half promised."

In the lounge were three people—Pamela, Grenville, and someone Burke had never met before. It was Delisle, and the Scotland Yard man was immediately interested. Here was Grenville's rival for the magnetic charms of Pamela Vance. It did not take Burke long to realise he was much older and certainly more sophisticated (especially when it came to women) than Grenville. The three were seated around the fire, talking.

Since Vance had been called away from his game of billiards and Delisle had learned that a detective from Scotland Yard had called he had been immensely curious. Delisle had not been slow in realising the significance of the letter Pamela had told him her father had received now that Scotland Yard were investigating the murder of Martin Stone—the very man Vance had been invited to murder. Delisle always said he liked to keep an open mind on such things, but what puzzled him was how Scotland Yard had been made aware of that letter Vance had received, for obviously Inspector Burke could have no other object for his visit to Blacon Grange.

Burke found himself being introduced to Delisle.

"Pamela tells me you're from Scotland Yard, Inspector?"

"I have that honour," confessed Burke, guardedly.

"I admire the Yard," went on Delisle sententiously. "Jolly efficient organisation. I hope you are successful in your quest, sir."

Burke smiled, but as he smiled he wondered how Delisle knew for what purpose he had come down to Blacon. Either the fellow was guessing or fishing, and in any event Burke had no intention of enlightening him. Instead he said: "Well, Ian, old chap, I'd better be getting back to the station. Remember what I said about the ten-thirty-three?"

Before Grenville could reply Delisle said: "You can manage that comfortably, Inspector, but if it's any help I can run you over in the car. I'm going myself now."

"Thanks for the thought, Mr. Delisle," smiled Burke, "but I have a fancy that the walk will do me good. Keep the weight down and all that, you know."

Burke shook hands cordially with Vance and his daughter and nodded genially to Delisle.

The pair of them had scarcely gone three paces down the drive than Burke halted suddenly. "I knew I'd forgotten something," he exclaimed in annoyance. "My gloves. I left them in the hall. Wait for me. I won't be more than a minute."

Burke raced up the steps of the house. He knew it was a crazy idea that had obsessed him ever since he had entered Blacon Grange, but he knew that he would not rest content until he had put it to the test.

Once again he faced the imperturbable Birtles at the door.

"I'm sorry to trouble you, Birtles," explained Burke, "but I find I've left my gloves behind. Somewhere in the hall, I think."

Birtles moved aside to allow Burke to pass, and the detective stood for a moment looking around him.

"Where did you have them last, sir?" asked the butler. "Perhaps you took them into the library?"

"No, Birtles, I quite definitely had them here. Ah," crossing swiftly to a table on which stood a large fern in an ornate bowl, "here they are."

But Burke had by no means finished. He turned to the butler ingenuously.

"Nice collection of knives, Birtles," he remarked, pointing to the weapon rack on the wall at the foot of the staircase. "I'm interested in weapons. Are you?"

"No, sir, I'm not," answered the butler emphatically. "Knives ought to be in their proper place—in the kitchen. That's a personal opinion, of course, you understand, sir."

"Perhaps it *is* in the kitchen, Birtles," remarked Burke slowly, eyeing the empty space at the bottom of the rack.

"I'm afraid I don't understand, sir."

"The one that is missing, Birtles! There is one missing, isn't there?"

Birtles gazed thoughtfully at the rack for a moment, then he turned slowly to the detective.

"Well, sir . . . I couldn't rightly say to be sure, sir. As I remarked, sir, I'm not particularly interested."

"Thanks, Birtles," said Burke, with just a trace of grimness in his tone. "Good-night!"

Grenville was strolling up and down the drive as Burke came up with him.

"Find your gloves?" he asked casually.

"Yes. . . . By the way, old man, does that offer of yours still hold good—about putting me up for the night, I mean?"

"Good lord, yes. But I say, what's the merry idea?" noting the sudden change in Burke's tone.

"I don't know," Burke announced thoughtfully, "and that's why I'm not catching the ten-thirty-three."

CHAPTER TEN

BURKE STAYS AT BLACON

GRANGE LODGE STOOD eastwards of Blacon village a pleasant little farmstead surrounded by trees.

Colonel Sir John Grenville was glad indeed when his son announced Detective Inspector Curtis Burke, for the colonel, despite his incapacity for farm management, due to physical infirmity which caused him to be wheeled around in an invalid chair, still held all his old-time respect for the law and for those who represented it.

Burke liked Sir John. He was typical of his generation . . . a county man if ever there was one: proud of his heritage.

But the baronet had to be early abed. His old batman, Jervis, who looked after him, was a martinet where his patient was concerned, and when it appeared as if Sir John was inclined to stay up until midnight chatting with Ian's old friend from Scotland Yard Jervis was firmness personified.

"Don't you think it's time, sir?" he asked quietly, as Sir John drained his glass for the third time.

Sir John looked helplessly at his son; then he grimaced at Burke.

"I don't know why I don't sack the fellow," he grumbled. "He orders me about as if he were my superior officer."

"At this time of night I am, sir," announced Jervis decisively.

"Oh, well," grumbled Sir John. "Good-night, Burke, and don't keep that son of mine out of his bed too long. He's got work to do early tomorrow."

When the door had closed Ian Grenville turned a troubled face to his friend. They were seated together over the big log fire that burned with a fierce red glow on the wide hearth of the snug little room.

"I want the truth, Curty, old man," he burst out impatiently. "What is the reason for your change of plan? Did you discover anything at Blacon Grange?"

Burke did not reply immediately. Very slowly he pressed down the tobacco into the brown bowl of his pipe. It was an action that suggested thoroughness, even in small things; as clear an indication of a man's character as anyone could wish. The man with the untidy, uncertain mind is always careless about the way he fills his pipe.

As soon as the pipe was drawing to the inspector's apparent satisfaction he looked across at Grenville.

"You've set me a difficult task in answering your questions," he began. "In the first place you know the reason for my unexpected visit to your little backwater. I came here to obtain information concerning the murder of Martin Stone, a London stockbroker. So far as I could ascertain from the slender material at my disposal there was only one man who could supply me with the information I wanted. That man was John Vance. As you know, I have seen Vance tonight. I asked him questions. His answers were perfectly satisfactory so far as I know. But," and here he paused reflectively, "there was one question I did not ask him. I wanted to see if he would volunteer the information, and I waited in vain. Perhaps I have erred in not pressing the question I particularly wanted answering. Perhaps I didn't.

"Did you notice that rack of old weapons—daggers and things—that hangs on the wall of the hall of Blacon Grange, close to the staircase?" Grenville nodded in a perplexed kind of way. He scarcely knew just what Burke was driving at, but he could tell by his tone that he was deadly serious.

"You did? Well, before Vance came out to us I noticed that one of the spaces was empty. I noticed that immediately because it is my job to notice things. I like things complete, and it struck me as curious that there should be a vacant place in that rack. It had once held a weapon of some sort. There was a slight mark where it had been. Don't ask me why I should be so infernally nosey. I can't tell you why that rack attracted my attention. It was just a stray idea presented to a straying eye, and in my line of business stray ideas are often valuable. Sometimes they present an altogether new line of inquiry."

Ian Grenville was staring steadfastly into the fire. He was interested, desperately interested, and did not interrupt as his friend proceeded to outline his impressions.

"To take matters chronologically," Burke went on smoothly, indeed almost lazily, as though he did not wish to break the spell that the warm fire laid upon them, "my chat with Vance was satisfactory up to a point. I knew that he had had dealings with Stone. I knew that Stone had, some years ago, been mixed up with a Mexican oil swindle in which quite a number of investors in this country had lost a considerable amount of money. In fact, I knew that Vance had written to one man whose name I do not yet know, advising him against touching the stock. When the affair went 'phut' that man wrote a nasty letter to Stone, in which he complained that he wished he had taken Vance's advice. That was how I became interested in John Vance.

"But there's something more important to it than that. Vance told me as much as he could remember about the affair. He told me he recollected answering inquiries about the venture made to him by some of his old clients. He could not, however, remember their names, but he is going to try to call them to mind. He did not tell me why on the day before his death Stone had scribbled on his memorandum tablet on his desk the words: 'Ring up Vance.' Now, Vance did not mention that telephone call tonight. Not a word about it. Can you think of any reason why he should riot disclose that important fact at a time when I—an official of Scotland Yard engaged on the investigation of a particularly foul murder—am questioning him regarding any associations he may have had with the man in question?"

Ian Grenville's eyes brightened. He had listened to Burke's story with eager interest. To his mind it was exciting. He could see exactly what the detective was driving at—that it was possible that someone who had fallen heavily financially in the bogus scheme of Stone's should have felt ill-inclined towards him and might even have plotted his death. The comment about the empty space in the dagger rack struck him as being at the moment beside the point. There was possibly some very good, probably quite trivial, explanation why Vance had not mentioned the alleged telephone call from Stone.

"But if Vance never received such a call, how could he tell you about it?" asked Grenville, with a distinct note of triumph in his voice. "I'm surprised at you for not thinking of that eventuality, Curty."

Curtis Burke smiled around the stem of his pipe and his eyes twinkled.

"I had thought of that, old man. I know for a certainty that the call was made."

"But how can you know that?"

"Listen! Before I came down here this afternoon I set my min-ions moving: I set them to inquire from the telephone exchange whether the call had been made and taken. Such inquiries do not take long. When the train stopped at Cheltenham a policeman was on the platform waiting for me with a message from Scotland Yard."

"But perhaps Vance never got the message," persisted Grenville, realising now the significance of the detective's argument.

"Oh, yes, he did. At least, the call was in operation long enough for him to have done so. If Vance did not receive it, someone else did and gave him the message. I cannot see anyone at the Grange, from Birtles downwards, omitting to mention a London call to the master. I am confident he got it. Believe me, old man, much as I hate to say it, Vance is holding something back, and that's the reason I have yielded to your kind offer to have me stay here to-night."

"What are you going to do?"

"I haven't made up my mind yet. One thing, however, is definite. I'm not going to force Vance's hand until I have to. In the morning I'm going to see him again. I want to know something about that collection of knives he's got there. They interest me, even if they don't apparently interest Birtles."

"Are you suggesting that Vance murdered Stone," asked Gren-ville, horrified.

"I'm not suggesting anything . . . just yet," said Burke grimly, "and I should advise you not to jump to conclusions either. We take little steps in our work, not whole flights of stairs. I've got a line, that's all, and in a case of this description some lines are lifelines; some of them are death-lines, too."

"What a ghoul you are, Curty," smiled Grenville with a mock shudder. "Your mind must be perpetually one big question mark. I suppose you've no line on me, by any chance? Really, I don't know how you can possibly have any friends."

"Don't be a fool," laughed Burke. "I'm sorry for your sake that I have to take this morbid interest, as you call it, in any friends of yours. By the way, I was forgetting, I agree whole-heartedly about Delisle. I don't like him any too well, either. He's too slick. A good-looker, undoubtedly . . . one of the type women so easily fall for, but all the same I think that if you were to dash in there you might very easily win. You see, old fellow, I used my eyes, and I noticed something in Pamela's face tonight when she caught sight of you that told me . . . well, I'm none too good at describing the peculiar love-light in a woman's eyes."

~ ~ ~ ~ ~

Up at Blacon Grange there was a confusion of thoughts.

Father and daughter sat together for a long time after Delisle had taken his departure. But it was far from being a silent sitting. Pamela was obviously shaken. Her face was paler than usual.

"Don't you think we should tell Mr. Burke about that letter, Daddy?" she asked.

Vance started. "My dear," he cried, "why should you think we should do that? Don't you see what might happen if this man Burke failed to discover the murderer of Stone? Have you never heard of circumstantial evidence?"

"But surely, Daddy, that's impossible. People can't be in two places at once. How could you have murdered a man in London. when all the time you were here?"

"I hadn't thought of that," said John Vance, excitedly. "Of course! But we mustn't say anything about that letter. D'you here, Pamela. Nothing!"

In his small room at the top of the house James Birtles sat on the edge of his bed with chin cupped in his hands and a frown on his forehead. He didn't like it. No. He didn't like it at all. Why should that detective come back for his gloves? He knew—Birtles knew. Just wanted to ask a question about the "knife rack." That was what it was and he, James Birtles, had nearly stumbled up on it.

No doubt Burke thought he was a smart fellow working that old gag about the gloves. Smart indeed! Birtles smiled to himself as he thought about it. It wasn't every day he had an opportunity of having the laugh on one of the "big five" or the "stupendous six," or whatever it was they called their clever selves, but Birtles had only just set that fern-pot down on the table a moment before Burke had rung the bell. He had brought it in from the dining-room, where it lived during the daytime.

Birtles chuckled to himself as he thought about it. But he was not at all sure why he laughed, because he knew that three days ago, when he had had to admonish Grace the maid about being careless with her dusting of the hall, the "knife rack" had possessed its full complement of weapons!

CHAPTER ELEVEN

VANCE DENIES EVERYTHING

EARLY THE FOLLOWING morning Burke presented himself at Blacon Grange and requested to see John Vance.

Burke knew that if Vance were at home their interview would not be interrupted, for on his way through the village he had seen Pamela Vance in the distance, trotting leisurely along on her horse.

John Vance expressed no surprise when Burke was shown into the room.

"So you didn't return to London, Mr. Burke?" Vance realised how superfluous the question was as soon as the words left his lips.

"Another thought crossed my mind as I was walking down to the village last night," the inspector explained. "It was so important that I decided to avail myself of Grenville's hospitality." Burke fixed the older man with a steady stare. "I forgot to ask you last night, Mr. Vance," he went on slowly, "whether on the morning of the day of the murder of Martin Stone you had a telephone message from him?"

"If I had done so, Mr. Burke, do you think I should have forgotten to mention that important fact to you last night?"

John Vance spoke slowly and evenly. There was no trace of excitement or apprehension in his voice, and Burke felt puzzled.

"That is a question only you can answer, Mr. Vance."

"And I have answered it." Vance smiled in a friendly way, but beneath the veneer was a tumult of emotions held skilfully in control. At all costs, he was telling himself, he must give nothing away—not so much by an inflexion of the voice or stirring of a muscle of his face must he betray himself.

"I think you ought to know that such a call was made from Stone's office," Burke told him.

John Vance appeared surprised. "You mean that a telephone call was made to me—here? Well, I suppose that is not impossible, but if that call came through it was not taken by me. I'll call Birtles and ask him, although it is most unlike Birtles to forget to give me a message."

Birtles came to them in response to the push of an electric bell.

"Mr. Burke says that a call was put through to here from London sometime during Tuesday morning, Birtles. Is that so, Birtles?"

The butler stood in silent contemplation for a moment. Then he shook his head.

"I took no such call, sir," he answered so emphatically that Burke believed the man to be speaking the truth.

"You are quite sure?" This from Burke.

"Quite sure, sir."

"Thank you, Birtles," said Vance, and when the man had gone, "You see Mr. Burke, I was quite right."

Curtis Burke was more puzzled than ever. There was something about Vance that compelled belief—either he was speaking the truth or he was an exceptionally clever liar.

"Well, I suppose we will have to leave that line of inquiry for the moment, Mr. Vance. Now there is another point I should like to clear up if I can. I notice in the hall that you have an admirable collection of old weapons. I saw them last night while Grenville and I were waiting. I noticed that one of the loops was empty. Can you tell me where the weapon is that should he there to complete that particular collection?"

Vance replied immediately: "Certainly. The collection is incomplete. I have gathered those weapons together over a period of years. Just how many I cannot tell you. When I had the rack made I utilised as much space as possible. If you had come here nine months ago you would have found three such empty spaces. Since then I have acquired two other examples—a Japanese dirk and an Indian example of a short-handled sacrifice knife. I rearranged my collection so that the empty place should be inconspicuous at the end of the row. I hope to be able some day to find another knife which will fill that particular rack. But tell me, Mr. Burke, why you should be so interested in that collection?"

"Simply because the weapon which killed Martin Stone has not yet been discovered." Burke spoke incisively. His words were as sharp as the weapons in the rack to which he alluded.

"I see. I can understand your interest, but I fear you are wasting your time. I am afraid I can assist you no further, Mr. Burke." Vance rose from his chair as though to end the interview.

The quick action rather startled the detective. He was asking himself why Vance should be in such a hurry for him to leave and immediately his senses were on the alert. Could it mean that his questions concerning the empty loop on the rack had momentarily unnerved this man of iron nerves, whose answers to his every question had been so calmly emphatic? Burke felt that his interest in Blacon Grange, if it had been mildly intriguing before, was now doubly so. There was a mystery here. He was certain of it. And it was a mystery which in some obscure way connected with the murder mystery he was unravelling.

Burke's next question, however, threw Vance from his guard with a completeness that was staggering.

"I presume, Mr. Vance, that you will have no objections to my putting a question or two to your servants?"

"This is monstrous, Mr. Burke. Are you not exceeding the limits of your authority?"

There was a noticeable tremor in the man's voice, and possibly there was fear in his eyes.

"If you mean have I a search warrant—no. I had been hoping that such a formality would not be necessary. Do I take it that your objection still holds good?"

"It certainly does. I should have thought, Mr. Burke, that you could have taken my word when I tell you that there is no weapon missing."

Burke elevated his eyebrows in surprise.

"It was not about that I particularly wished to question your staff, Mr. Vance," he said. "I was wondering whether someone else might not have taken that telephone message."

A look of intense relief flashed into John Vance's eyes—a look which did not pass unnoticed by the watchful Burke.

"That, of course, is rather different, Mr. Burke. I will have them brought here at once if you wish."

But Burke surprised him by his reply. "I rather think I've changed my mind, sir. I will postpone the ordeal for the present. Perhaps it will not be necessary after all."

"I'm glad to hear you say that, but if it will help you at all I'll instruct Birtles to question the maids, the cook and the gardeners about it, but I'm afraid it will yield nothing because . . . well, if such a call had been put through and had been taken by any member of my staff it would most certainly have been brought to my notice."

Burke's first place of call on leaving Blacon Grange was at Blacon police station. It was not an imposing building . . . just an ordinary cottage with the county constabulary sign in a blue and white plaque over the door.

A pink-cheeked woman opened the door in response to his knock, and Burke asked to see the sergeant.

"Sergeant's busy just now," she told him. "Is it urgent, sir?"

Burke told her it was, and to emphasise his words he handed her his official card and asked her to present it to the sergeant with his compliments.

The pink-cheeked woman stared at the card for a full minute.

"You be from Scotland Yard, sir?" she asked incredulously. Burke nodded and smiled as he watched her disappear within without another word.

Almost immediately the sergeant appeared. He was minus his tunic—a large, well-made country bobby with a complexion like a ripe apple.

"Come inside, sir. Martha had no right to keep you awaitin' like this."

"She told me you were busy, Sergeant," smiled Burke, "but I don't think my business will keep you many minutes."

Sergeant Mulliver led the way inside. They passed through the tidy living-room into a room at the back, which presumably served the purpose of lock-up and charge-room. Its furnishings consisted of a plain deal-topped table, three straight-backed wooden chairs and a tall desk beside the window that overlooked the garden at the back.

When the door was closed Sergeant Mulliver turned a pair of wondering eyes on his visitor, still holding between his clumsy fingers the small piece of pasteboard that Burke had presented.

"Well, Sergeant," began Burke, "let's get down to business. As you see, I'm from Scotland Yard—a rare visitor to this part of the world. But I'm not here on a holiday. I'm investigating a murder—a rather nasty murder, Sergeant. You've heard about it in the general report. I mean Martin Stone who was murdered in London on Wednesday night. I want to find the murderer, and that's why I must have your help."

This announcement was too much for Mulliver. He stood staring at Burke as if he had been an apparition.

"Me, sir," he stuttered. "You want me to help. . . . Holy snakes, sir, what can I do? You're not here atellin' me that the murderer's in Blacon, eh, are you?"

"Now, Sergeant, I don't want any excitement. I always understood that the county constabulary were a calm body of men and that their sergeants were always equal to any emergency."

Sergeant Mulliver literally pulled himself together. He reached over to a hook behind the closed door and lifted down his tunic, which he donned hastily.

"At your service, sir."

"That's better," commended the detective, as he seated himself on one of the straight-backed chairs. "Now listen! What's the strength at Blacon?"

"One sergeant and one constable, sir."

"Does that constable know the area well and, more important, does he know the people?"

"Every man jack of 'em, sir. And not a few of the wenches." Mulliver winked with a large and expressive eye. "Beggin' your pardon, sir!"

"That's fine," Burke told him. "What time will your constable be showing up?"

"He's due any minute now, sir. On cycle patrol, he is. That's the only way we can get around these parts."

Burke drummed on the edge of the table with his finger-tips. Much as he liked Sergeant Mulliver, it was not his intention to give much away concerning his visit to Blacon. There might come a time when he would have much more work for Mulliver and his constable than he had at the moment.

"Anything I can do, sir?" Mulliver's voice sounded refreshingly eager.

"Not just yet, Mulliver—not until I've seen your constable."

A minute or two later Constable Cummings reported to the sergeant.

"This is the constable, sir."

Burke regarded the newcomer with interest. He was tall and young and had brown, curly hair . . . just the sort of policeman to ingratiate himself with the servants at Blacon Grange.

"Good morning, Constable. I wonder if you know anyone up at Blacon Grange?"

"You mean Mr. Vance and Miss Pamela, sir?"

Burke shook his head. "I mean the servants—the women servants."

Constable Cummings never remembered blushing before in the whole of his professional career, but at Burke's words he was conscious of a crimson flood-tide sweeping his face and neck, and he was conscious also that Burke and the sergeant had noticed it, too.

"In a manner of speaking, I do, sir—yes. I hope there's nothing wrong. . . ."

"So do I," smiled Burke. "But you haven't told us who it is at Blacon Grange you do know."

"I was coming to that, sir. It's Grace—Grace Jervis, the parlourmaid. I've known her for the past eighteen months, sir."

"And when will you be seeing her again?"

"I could go along now, if you like, sir, couldn't I, Sergeant?"

"He certainly could, Mr. Burke, if there's anything you're wanting."

"That's just what I want to avoid. I don't want any policeman in uniform hanging around the house. When do you usually see her, Cummings?"

"Well, sir, it's her afternoon out this afternoon, and I could make it my business to see her if you so desired. She lives down the street, sir."

"Then I can count on you seeing the young lady and asking her a few questions, eh?"

"You certainly can, sir."

And for the next few minutes Burke was busy telling Constable Cummings just what it was. he wanted to know about Blacon Grange from Grace Jervis.

CHAPTER TWELVE

PAMELA LEARNS THE TRUTH

PAMELA VANCE WAS not happy as she cantered over the bracken-clad hill alone.

A few days ago she had been remarkably happy and free from care. Today she felt as if a dark cloud had settled about her, blacking out the sunshine. And it had all come about as a result of that letter her father had received.

She wanted to think—wanted to be alone to think. It wasn't as if she hadn't been thinking pretty deeply these past few days, and now on top of all this worry with her father and the mystery of Martin Stone's murder, Rodney Delisle was pestering her for an answer to his question of an engagement to marry him.

Under less abnormal circumstances she would probably have been less miserable, but she felt that her future was bound up with her father more than she had ever imagined. She knew him too well not to understand what he was suffering, and the visit of Inspector Burke last night had not improved matters. In fact, the appearance of the Scotland Yard man seemed to have precipitated a minor crisis. Her father, of course, could not have murdered that man, despite the letter of invitation he had received. That was quite impossible. But there was no knowing what this man Burke might not find out. If he found out about the letter Pamela was sensible enough to realise that Burke might take a great deal of convincing that the coincidence was as absurd as they wished him to think.

Added to this, she was not yet too sure that she wanted to be married to Rodney Delisle, much as she liked and admired him. In her mind arose a picture of Ian Grenville. Ian had always had a place in her heart, even if it was only a corner. And there was the possibility that people might move out of the obscurity of corners into the centre of the room!

Thoughts of Ian gave her a new angle to one of her perplexities. Burke was a friend of Ian's. Why shouldn't she go over to Grange

Lodge and see if Ian knew anything more than Burke had told her father?

Pamela turned her horse towards the eastward valley. It was not yet noon and there was just a chance that Ian was to be found somewhere on the estate.

She found him standing—disconsolately, she thought—in the centre of the old clover meadow, staring at a gap in a broken hedgerow. He swung around swiftly as he heard the clop-clop of the horse's hooves on the soft ground.

Pamela dropped lightly from the saddle and stood holding the bridle.

"Hello, Ian. Meditating on the glories of Nature again. Do you ever do any real work?"

"I'm just wondering when to start the job of repairing that hedge," he told her. "That's the fifth time in three months it's been broken down. Looks to me as if someone was using it as a short cut from the lane. It's the thinnest part, you see, and the gate's too far over to be of service to anyone coming along the main Blacon-Hereford road."

But Pamela was scarcely listening to the young man's conversation. She didn't want to talk about hedgerows and broken briars.

"Where's your detective friend?" she ventured. "Did he return to town last night?"

Ian's eyes turned to her sharply. It wasn't often that Pamela sought him out as she had done now—at least, not since Delisle had become a neighbour. And swiftly there arose in his mind once again what Burke had told him last night.

"No, he's still here somewhere," he told her. "I asked him to stay for the night. He's an awfully decent fellow, old Curty, you know."

"I don't know why he should want to bother Daddy," she said. "He's quite upset about it. Does Mr. Burke really expect to find the murderer in Blacon?"

"I don't know," Grenville told her quietly. "He was talking about it last night, but being a detective he didn't tell me very much. Detectives don't confide even in their oldest friends."

He noticed the sudden look of disappointment on the girl's sensitive face.

"I'm awfully sorry, Pam," he said quickly. "I'd do anything I could to help you—you know that, and I'm just as worried about this thing as probably you are yourself. But do you know what I really do think?" A hopeful gleam returned to the girl's eyes. "I think that, for once old Curtis is barking up the wrong tree. You see, it's hard on him in this case not to have very much to go on. He's had to pick up the crumbs where and when he could, but people with clean consciences have never any real occasion to worry."

"Why should you say that?" Pamela ejaculated almost breathlessly.

For a moment he gazed at her amazed. She was a puzzle this morning with a vengeance. He had never known her like this.

"Isn't it true?" he countered. "Scotland Yard doesn't manufacture evidence. This is England, not America."

If only she dare tell him the truth—tell him of her wild 'suspicions; tell him about that letter and her father's mysterious behaviour on the night the crime was committed! But she knew that she could not do that. She had promised her father that she would not tell a soul. And if she did break that promise and reveal it to Ian—Ian was a friend of Curtis Burke and Ian was one of those sticklers for truth and justice and all that sort of thing; admirable virtues under normal circumstances; but of little use today, as she understood the position. Pamela's moral sense seemed to have become somewhat blunted since the receipt of that disastrous letter.

"You don't know where Mr. Burke is this morning, then?" The question came in the nature of an anti-climax—an evasion of the point at issue.

Grenville looked at her, torn between his love for her and his loyalty to his friend. Yet what could it matter now if he told her? By this time Burke would probably have seen John Vance, and if Pamela didn't know, it meant that she had left Blacon Grange before Burke's arrival.

"He went to see your father."

The colour fled from the girl's cheeks. Her hands twitched nervously at the animal's bridle.

"Why?" she asked. "Why should he go worrying Daddy again? Wasn't last night sufficient?" Her voice rose to an agonising crescendo that alarmed him.

"I really don't know, Pam," he lied awkwardly. "He didn't say. It must have been something he forgot to ask him last night. After all, it's only some sort of information about Stone's business he wants. Hundreds of people must have come into contact with Stone, and your father just happens to be one of them. It's not important."

Pamela Vance looked hard into the young man's face.

"You're lying to me, Ian Grenville," she challenged coldly. "You know you are lying. You're in league with that man—and I always believed you were my friend."

Consternation flooded Grenville's mind and imagination. He felt trapped. Yet he had no intention of telling her everything Burke had told him last night.

"I'm sorry if you think that, Pam," he managed to blurt out. "Some day perhaps you will understand."

With a look of scorn mingled with the utmost contempt she leapt into the saddle and without so much as a second glance turned the horse's head towards Blacon. He watched her, aware that his eyes were suspiciously moist—watched her take the low fence on the far side of the field . . . until she was out of sight.

Pamela found her father pacing up and down the sunlit lounge. He stopped as she entered.

"Had a good canter?" he smiled.

"Good enough until I heard that that detective had been worrying you again."

Vance looked surprised. "Who told you that?"

"Ian Grenville. What did he want?"

"He wanted to question the servants about a dagger that is missing from the rack in the hall."

Pamela stared at her father open-mouthed. Then she recovered her composure and ran swiftly from the room. In a moment she returned, and there was a look on her face that Vance hoped he would never see there again.

"He was right," she said calmly. "There is one missing."

He nodded. "I know—now."

"What has happened to it—where is it?" she cried desperately, clutching the lapels of his coat and staring wildly into his face.

"I don't know." The words came in a hoarse whisper from his dry lips.

There were hot tears in her eyes and they scorched their way down her cheeks.

"Daddy! Daddy!" she sobbed brokenly. "Say it isn't true. You didn't kill him, did you?"

Vance drew his daughter close to him until her wet face was buried in his shoulder. With one hand he stroked her hair.

"Calm, my darling. Calm! You know I didn't— that I couldn't."

The girl continued to sob convulsively. Then she drew away from him and straightened herself.

"Does Burke suspect anything about that letter?" she asked.

"I did not mention it."

"What did you tell him about the missing dagger?" The question caused him his first moment of real panic that day.

"I told him that there never had been one there—that I was hoping to secure one some day."

"But why did you tell him that?" The girl was becoming wild again. If only she had not gone for her ride!

Vance was silent for a moment. He felt that the time had come when he could no longer keep the secret to himself. He must tell Pamela the truth—as far as he knew it.

When he had finished his story she lay back in the folds of the chair, staring at him wide-eyed. But she believed him. She understood him now as she had never understood him before. She knew the agony and the torture he had endured these past few hours, and she admired him for the stiff upper lip he had kept. But she knew, too, that there was danger.

Her father's story could not be corroborated. That was where he had made the fatal mistake. But she realised how essential it was that Curtis Burke should never know the truth. There was circumstantial evidence. If Burke got to know about that letter and the fact that her father had actually gone to see Stone that fateful night . . . had actually found him dead . . . killed with the missing dagger from his collection in the hall. . . . Her thoughts were a nightmare.

"We've got to stick together, Daddy. We've got some deadly unseen enemy and we need each other's help. Not long ago Ian said something about clean consciences. I guess he's right, even though I was mad with him at the time. We've just got to sit tight and say nothing."

"But Burke wants to question the servants, remember."

Pamela rose from her chair. "I'll go and see them myself. They'll do—and say—anything for me."

Unprotesting Vance watched her go. He knew it was tampering with justice; that she might be punished. Perhaps he should not have told her . . . should not have burdened her with such a secret. But he was weak, pitiably weak after the strain of the last few days and the temptation to confide in some sympathetic ear had been irresistible. Fate had driven him into a corner. It was neither his fault nor his crime. Surely he and Pamela were entitled to take what measures they considered best to protect themselves.

He looked at his watch. It was nearly one o'clock. He did not feel in the least hungry.

Pamela returned a few minutes later.

"I've spoken to them—and told them what to say," she declared triumphantly. "All of them except Grace," she added. "It's her half-day, and Birtles let her go off at twelve o'clock. She's going over to Gloucester shopping. But I'll see her tonight. Burke won't be able to get her before then."

In the middle of lunch the telephone bell rang. It was a call for Pamela. Instantly she recognised Delisle's voice.

"Thought you said you were going up to Town this morning?" she questioned, surprised.

"I had intended," came back the reply, "but I've put it off until next week. By the way, Pam, I want to see you this afternoon. Everything all right?"

"Yes—I think so," she hesitated.

"It's important."

"You sound very serious."

"I am serious. I've been thinking things over—about that letter, you know, and with Scotland Yard on the job down here I think it would be best to tell Inspector Burke about it."

"Rodney," the girl almost screamed. "Not that! You mustn't do that. You mustn't."

His voice came back calm and unhurried. "And why not? It would be better to mention it rather than that Burke should discover it? He'd think then that you really had something to hide."

"But how could he find out about the letter?" Pamela's heart was beating furiously.

"Burke's a clever fellow, so I'm told. Where can I see you, Pam?"

"Anywhere. Anywhere at all!"

"Good! I'll run round in the car and bring you across to my place, then we can talk things over."

The girl hung up the receiver with nerveless fingers.

This was the second crisis today, but nevertheless she felt confident that she could make Rodney Delisle see the folly of his suggestion and there would be no need to worry her father about it.

CHAPTER THIRTEEN

MORE CLUES

CURTIS BURKE RETURNED to London by the two o'clock train. He felt that he had done all he could usefully manage for the moment at Blacon. He had left an instruction with Sergeant Mulliver to telephone him any report which Constable Cummings might bring in as a result of his conversation with Grace Jervis, the parlour-maid.

On his arrival at Scotland Yard he reported to his superintendent and was told that the assistant commissioner, Sir Michael Kenyon, wished to see him.

Sir Michael was a policeman. He understood the difficulties of routine work as well as anyone, and he knew that if nothing tangible had so far resulted from Inspector Burke's investigations of the murder of Martin Stone it would not be Burke's fault.

Burke gave the assistant commissioner a *précis* of the case, leaving nothing out—not even his suspicions that John Vance, retired and wealthy stockbroker of Blacon Grange, was not telling everything he knew.

When he had ended the commissioner looked thoughtful.

"There's nothing known against Vance at all, you say? Any idea of his early history?"

"No, nothing at all. He appears to have been a model of propriety in every respect."

"Yet you suspect him of not telling the whole truth?"

"At the moment, sir, yes," answered Burke firmly. "I am awaiting a report from Blacon. It depends largely on that report how soon I pay a second visit."

"It certainly looks as if that is the right end. So far as I can gather from the information we have been able to gather here, only the telephone call to Blacon appears to possess any significance. If Vance denies having received it he is either telling the truth or else he has a jolly good reason for remaining quiet about it. The Exchange says that there is not the slightest doubt that it was accepted at the Blacon end and that the call was an effective one."

Sir Michael's voice had a sharp ring to it, and Burke was not slow to understand the significance. "Have you checked up Vance's movements on the day of the crime?"

"Not yet, sir. You understand I have been in a rather delicate position for the past twenty-four hours. I have been working largely on conjecture. After all, it was a very slender pretext to question the man on at all."

"I agree with you, Burke, but, as I say, I am confident that Vance knows more about this affair than he is letting us know. He may have very good reasons for that, and one of those reasons is that he may be shielding someone."

"I've thought all that out, sir, and if I get a positive report from the station at Blacon I shall have more authority for pushing my interrogation further."

Sir Michael pulled his six feet of height out of his deep-seated swivel-chair.

"I'm relying on you, Burke. You've never let me down and I don't think you are going to record your first failure over this case."

The interview closed on a note of optimism for Curtis Burke. Sir Michael was a particularly shrewd man who knew what he was talking about.

Arriving at his own desk, he found the report for which he was waiting. It ran: "Cummings interviewed the girl Jervis, who is willing to swear that a week ago the rack of weapons was complete. Am awaiting instructions."

Burke felt elated. It had been a long shot with a bow drawn at a venture, but it had hit the target. Immediately he lifted his desk telephone and informed Sir Michael.

"I'm going down first thing tomorrow morning," he added, and Sir Michael voiced his approval.

In the meantime Curtis Burke was not idle. Much work had been done in his absence. His subordinates, too, had done that work well. Mr. Rodgers, for instance, Stone's chief clerk, had, under the guidance of a police officer, made a diligent and competent search of the firm's files in reference to the Mexican oil swindle and a long list of names and addresses awaited the detective's scrutiny and consideration.

Burke was particularly interested in that list and gave immediate instructions for his staff to discover the movements on the day of the crime of a dozen or more persons whose addresses were more readily accessible. But if Burke had been excited a moment ago at the news he had received from Blacon, he was even more elated as he went through the list. There were two names there that caused him to purse his lips in a whistle of surprise. One of them was Colonel Sir John Grenville and the other Mr. Rodney Delisle.

Here were two names he had never expected to find, but what was even more curious, both of them lived at Blacon. Of course, it was absurd to suspect Sir John of being in the least implicated. Sir John Grenville was an invalid who was wheeled about in a chair. But Delisle presented an altogether different problem. Delisle was a friend of Pamela Vance and of her father. He was Ian Grenville's rival for the affections of that young lady and Ian Grenville had said that he considered him a bounder.

Curtis Burke felt that his next visit to Blacon was going to be an interesting one. On the other hand, he argued, it would be foolish of him to leap to conclusions. Any one or perhaps more than one person named on that list had a motive for the murder of Martin Stone. But why had they waited so long? From the information he had been able to gather about the Mexican oil swindle as he referred to it in his notes, the crash had come three years ago. These people had lost sums varying in amounts from a few pounds to a few thousand. It was a pity that friend Rodgers had not been able to discover the amounts of their individual losses.

That information would have been particularly helpful. Yet, as it was, he congratulated himself on these discoveries. He was making progress. Yet, somehow, the longer he thought over the case the more he was disinclined to believe that John Vance was the murderer. Similar thoughts crossed his mind as regards Sir John Grenville and Rodney Delisle. Despite the fact that Ian Grenville disliked the fellow, Burke was a fairly shrewd judge of character himself, and so far as he was concerned Delisle had impressed him as being a man—somewhat cynical it was true—scarcely capable of such a diabolical murder.

Before he left Scotland Yard Burke had an interview with the Press representatives. They wanted their inevitable story. For four days they had had to be content with the crumbs that fell from the commissioner's table. As for the rest, they had to scratch about for themselves and the marvel of it was that they had succeeded in setting forth a number of perfectly feasible but nevertheless garish stories and theories concerning the case.

With the return of Curtis Burke they knew that he would deal more leniently with them, and they were not disappointed. Burke had his own particular axe to grind. He regaled them with the theory that the murder had been committed by someone who, three years

previously, had lost a considerable sum of money in a rather unsavoury stock market swindle emanating from America and having
its tentacles in some fabulous Mexican oil wells. The story sounded
good. But what was more important from Burke's point of view
was the request that Scotland Yard would be glad to hear from
anyone who had lost money in the scheme. He was careful enough,
however, to imply that the Yard was not for one moment suggesting
that Martin Stone was to blame for this hocus. He went so far as to
infer that Stone had doubtless handled the prospectus in all good
faith and that no one had been more grieved than he that the affair
had turned out to be a "frost."

It was the old, old example of *de mortuis*, with the official seal of
Scotland Yard attached to the wreath. Burke's object in putting the
matter this wise was the hope that he might be able to get into touch
with someone who could supply certain information about the
murdered man's activities in relation to these decidedly "shady"
affairs. For all Burke knew there might have been others—others
which that rat-like individual Mr. Rodgers had conveniently forgotten.

As a personality, Burke did not think too highly of Mr. Rodgers,
and a detective had, since the date of the murder, been told off to
check up that gentleman's movements. So far Mr. Rodgers had
remained faithful to his home, apart from police-conducted tours of
Stone's offices and his own occasional perambulations around the
coffee-houses frequented by stock-jobbers and their fry who might,
so it was presumed, be able to put him into touch with further employment.

The next morning, when Curtis Burke set off by road to Blacon,
he had the satisfaction of noticing that most of the morning newspapers had given revived prominence to Scotland Yard's new theory regarding the "Office Murder."

CHAPTER FOURTEEN

DELISLE'S THREATS

THE HOUSE THAT Rodney Delisle rented just beyond the cloistered rim of Blacon village was small and quite unpretentious. In its way it was attractive. Its double-fronted aspect was clothed luxuriously with Virginian creeper that, at this season of the year, was a blaze of fiery scarlet.

For Delisle's "Virginian Cottage" was more in the nature of a summer retreat than a permanent residence. During the autumn and the winter he occupied a service flat in Jermyn Street. At Blacon he was attended by a daily woman, Jessica Foulkes, from the village, and also by a manservant, by name Sydney Grainger, who was apparently something in the nature of a chauffeur-gardener.

Pamela had met him once or twice. On her London visits in the company of Delisle it was Grainger who invariably drove them. On this afternoon when Delisle had driven her across to the cottage the girl was quick to notice that Grainger was absent, and commented on that fact.

"I've sent Sydney up to Town for a few oddments," Delisle explained, "and since I wanted the car myself he's gone up by train."

Pamela had to be satisfied with the explanation, but nevertheless there was something that instinctively warned her that the absence of Grainger was singularly odd.

Delisle had installed her in an easy chair in the well-appointed sitting-room and he noticed that she was obviously nervous. She had removed her gloves, but held them in her hands, fingering them absently.

On the way to the cottage she had broached the subject of his telephone message, but he had sidetracked her with the remark that there was plenty of time for that discussion, and that a motor-car was not an ideal venue for conversation.

"I do wish you would tell me what you mean, Rodney?" she asked anxiously. "You really did give me a fright over the 'phone."

Delisle stood with his back to the fire that glowed invitingly in the small low grate. He appeared perfectly composed as he smoked his cigarette.

"I'm afraid, my dear," he began calmly, "that we have got to face facts, and I want you to realise that it is only after a great deal of serious thought that I have brought you here to discuss the matter. I realise it was nice of you to confide in me about the letter. Under the circumstances I consider you did perfectly right in not keeping it a secret from me. At the time," he went on, "I, too, regarded the affair as a stupid practical joke. What else could any of us have regarded it? But I'm sure, Pamela, you must realise as well as I do that in view of what has happened, your father is in a curiously awkward position, and if that Scotland Yard detective, Burke, hadn't come nosing about down here, I agree that to say the least about it was all for the best." He paused, apparently watching the effect of his words on the girl. Then he proceeded:

"But things are different now. Burke is one of those fellows who stick at nothing to get at the truth, and I fear that, sooner or later, he will get to know about that letter. When he does, think what the position of your father will be. In his silence concerning it Burke will immediately jump to the conclusion that your father knows more about the murder that he has seen fit to disclose in his conversations with Burke. Now I figure it out this way. If Burke is told about that letter things won't look quite so black against your father as they will if Burke had to ferret out the facts for himself."

"How do you mean—look black for Father?" Pamela tried desperately hard to keep an appearance of calm in her voice, but she realised only too well that she was not being too successful.

Delisle regarded the girl with serious eyes.

"My dear Pamela, surely you are sensible enough to appreciate the seriousness of your father's position. Here we have a man receiving a letter instructing him to murder a certain person. He laughs at the idea. He regards it as a preposterous joke. Then comes the news that that person has actually been murdered. I ask you, Pamela, in the absence of any further tangible clue to the murderer, what is Scotland Yard to think, and more particularly if he cannot give a satisfactory account of his movements on the night the crime was committed?"

"But he can, Rodney!" Pamela protested hotly. "You were there when he came in . . . you heard what he said . . . where he had been. . . ."

Pamela felt as if she were being driven into a corner. She had never for a moment suspected that Delisle would take such an "official" view of the affair as he seemed to be doing.

A curious smile played around the man's lips.

"Do you really believe that story about his driving around the Herefordshire and Gloucestershire lanes admiring the brilliance of the stars? Don't you see we have only his word for that— uncorroborated? Really, Pamela, I don't want to appear a brute, but as I said before, we have got to face facts, and it is because I care for you so very much that I don't want either you or your father to do anything silly. If he is innocent he need have no fear, so why protest that we need keep silent about that letter?"

The girl's face had grown very white—white as the gloves she so nervously played with in her lap. Her lips felt oddly dry, and she was conscious of the furious nature of her heart-beats. This man was talking as if her father was guilty—as if. . . . Pamela hardly trusted herself to reply to him.

"You don't believe Father, then?" Her words were uttered almost in a frightened whisper. Then came back the challenging retort:

"Do you, my dear Pamela?"

For the moment the girl was dumb. How dare this man talk like this to her? Was he doubting her loyalty to her father? Was he seriously suggesting that she—she, Pamela Vance—was in league with her parent to defeat the ends of that justice he was presuming to defend? The situation was becoming preposterous, and had it been anyone other than Rodney Delisle she would have known how to deal with him.

She retorted: "Of course I do. No matter what you may try to imply to the contrary, my father had nothing whatever to do with the death of this man. I shall be ready to swear to that."

"I fear we are becoming unnecessarily melodramatic," he told her. "Also we appear to be wandering somewhat from the point at issue. As I told you over the telephone, I am torn between two lines of action. The first is whether to divulge the secret of your father's letter to Burke or whether, in your own interest—or should I say *our* interests?—it might be better to say nothing at all. That is the problem we have to solve. It is a matter, Pamela, between our two selves. Now which is it going to be?"

"I fail to see that it is only our concern," she answered quietly. "I think that Daddy ought to be consulted. After all, it is his affair—far more his affair in fact that it is either of ours."

Then, quite suddenly, the man took an altogether new line.

"I suppose you know, Pamela, that I love you very much?"

"You've told me so many times, Rodney, but I don't think this is quite the moment for reiteration." There was a softer note in the girl's voice.

"That's where you're wrong," he exclaimed, breathing quickly as he took a stride towards her and gripped her fiercely by the shoulders. "This *is* the time to talk about it. I want you, Pamela —I've wanted you for months. And for months you've vacillated. You're in love with me—you know you are. Every time I see you I am made more and more aware of it. Young Grenville means nothing to you. He's only a simpering loon—unworthy of a woman so vibrant with life as you are. . . ."

"Don't! Please, Rodney, don't!" protested Pamela hysterically.

"You've got to hear me," he answered her fiercely, and she felt his fingers like twin talons in the soft warm flesh of her shoulders. "I've got to have your answer—d'you hear, your answer—now. Will you marry me, Pamela? Promise me you will do that?"

The girl was sobbing brokenly. The man must be heartless to trouble her with so vital a question at a time like the present. He must be mad. Perhaps he was—made mad with his love for her. For one fleeting moment Pamela believed that extraneous circumstances did not matter in so personal an affair. But the next moment she knew she was wrong. Her whole life was bound up in the happiness of her father; and her father was in danger. Self must be sacrificed for his sake and for his safety.

"Can't you give me a little longer time to think it over, Rodney?" she pleaded softly. "You're asking me to do such a big thing. I can't tell you yet—honestly I can't."

She looked into his face as it bent down towards her. His emotions were unleashed. There was a metallic glitter in his dark eyes and his breathing quickened.

"You've got to decide now," he told her. "I'm not going to be played with a moment longer. I'm no longer the mouse—I'm the cat—the animal reverted if you like to its jungle days. I want your answer. I'm waiting."

Pamela was desperately afraid. This was a new man who stood over her. The sound of the threat in his voice scared her. It was as though someone had suddenly scratched through the veneer.

"And what if I refuse to give you an answer, Rodney?" Her voice was a quivering challenge.

"I was forgetting," he answered her more calmly, "there is an alternative. Either you promise to marry me or—I hate to say it, Pamela—I may feel disposed to stifle my private conscience and acquaint Burke with the knowledge I possess concerning a certain invitation to murder which your father recently received and which he has not yet thought fit to divulge to the police."

The girl recoiled from him, horror frozen in her eyes. He stood back a pace from her, watching, waiting. She struggled to her feet, clutching her gloves. The mask was gone.

"Do you know what you are saying?" she cried in anguish.

He nodded. "Yes! I know it sounds revolting to you, but you've driven me to it and now—now I don't care. I'm desperate—desperate, I tell you. What is your answer?"

"If I see Mr. Burke on my return through the village I shall tell him you have something to say to him." She flung the words at him scornfully.

Rodney Delisle felt momentarily defeated. The girl had proved not quite so easy as he had imagined. She had spirit—plenty of spirit. The sight of her face as she spoke goaded him to action. He took a quick pace forward and seized her wrists.

"Not yet!" he exclaimed. "You don't seem to realise just what your decision means. Have you forgotten what I have already told you? Remember there are many men who have stepped on to the gallows as a result of circumstantial evidence less strong than the evidence in the present case."

The man's words made her pause. There was a difference in his tone. It was more pleading, more human. Its emotional edge had been dulled.

Slowly she began to appreciate that what he was telling her was the truth. It would never do for Burke to believe her father to be in the smallest degree implicated in the crime he was investigating. To become aware of that letter meant the beginning oi an inquiry which might, as Delisle had hinted, end on the scaffold.

Pamela shuddered. If she had possessed any feeling; any sentiment for Delisle before, she had none now. Her emotions for him were dead. He had murdered them.

"Perhaps I have been hasty," she managed to admit. "I was forgetting. I accept your—terms, Mr. Delisle, but I stipulate this: There will be no marriage until the murderer of Martin Stone is brought to judgment."

The man regarded her with smiling curiosity. He had won and he could afford to be magnanimous.

"And what if he is never discovered? What then?"

"He will be discovered."

"You appear very confident of that!"

"Perhaps I am! Do you accept that?" she asked impatiently.

"I have no alternative," he smiled, bowing gallantly.

CHAPTER FIFTEEN

TWO MEN TALK

THAT NIGHT IN "The Crown," a public-house in the neighbourhood of Sweeting Steps in that wharf-infested area of the Thames at Wapping, there were two drunken men.

This was not an unusual sight in "The Crown," where lightermen and others congregated and where seamen from the ships that swung their bow-lights out in mid-stream dropped in for a drink or two.

One of the men, who was obviously drunk, seemed oddly out of place there. His dress and his general appearance more betokened a suburban hotel. He wore a brown tweed overcoat and a bowler hat. Beneath the turn-ups of his pin-stripe trousers there peeped a pair of grey spats.

He had been "having a few" before he pushed open the brass-railed single swing door of "The Crown," but in the opinion of the potman, whose judgment on such delicate matters was irrefutable, he was quite fit to be served with more.

The man sat down majestically on a torn leather-covered bench beside a beer-slopped table, deposited his glass and looked around him. He wanted to talk; but he had no desire to talk to himself. A few feet away from him were four or five sailormen and a bargee hobnobbing over their pots. When one of them glanced across in his direction the newcomer nodded with that geniality which is common to a certain stage of inebriation. The group apparently decided that the stranger's company was not for them, and continued their yarning.

It was just then that another stranger lurched along—a stranger, that is, to the potman and the "regulars." But to the man who had just seated himself this second man, obviously much worse for drink than he was himself, was indeed a friend in a strange land, and he immediately indicated that the gentleman should occupy a seat beside him.

The newcomer swayed slightly and gripped the edges of the table for support.

"Half a mo', matey," cautioned the man who was seated, "drop yer rusty anchor here aside o' me. That's better," as the intoxicated one dropped heavily on to the bench.

"Wot chavin'?" Despite the thickness of the other's speech the genial gentleman interpreted the request with remarkable accuracy.

"How about a pint o' bitter, eh?"

"Suits me," commented the second man, beckoning to the bartender.

Half an hour later it was rather surprising to find that the intoxicated one was neither better nor worse than he had been when first he had entered "The Crown"; but the first man, who had begun by being politely genial, was now boastingly voluble. To him talking was a necessity, and it appeared that he told the second man that what he mostly wanted was to forget. Just what it was he wished to dissociate from his memory was not at all clear, but after a while he began to grow more confidential.

"You've heard about this murder in the City, eh?"

The second man nodded his head sagely.

"Well," continued the first man, "they've had me up at Scotland Yard. What-cher think o' that? I'll bet choove never bin in Scotland Yard?" The other shook his head sadly.

"Wot you tellin' me all this for?" protested the listener. "You'll be tellin' me next that you knows the bloke what done 'im in."

The first speaker, still more confidentially, leaned a little closer.

"P'raps I could, Mister. And again—p'raps I couldn't, see!"

"Wot's Scotland Yard like?" asked the second man, in a burst of interest. "Did they grill yer?"

"Not arf they didn't. Third degree stuff. But I'm tough, baby! Gee! I'm tough!"

"I should say you are," complimented the other. "I'd like ter bet not many come out of it half so well, eh? 'Nother drop o' short?"

"This is on me," protested the first man. "You're my guest. Didn't I invite yer to sit dahn 'ere? Course I did. But listen. That bloke what got himself murdered arsked for it, 'e did. The mean, dirty little skunk. I tells yer, I'm glad 'e's gorn. Cheerio!"

They sat on for a few minutes longer before they departed. The first man lurched along the road towards the river bridge; the other man, surprisingly sober, watched his erstwhile friend depart. Then he did a rather amazing thing. He entered a nearby telephone booth and dialled Whitehall 1212.

"Is that the Yard? Put me on to Sergeant Forster. . . . That you, Sergeant? Rafter speaking. I've just left Rodgers; he's been drinking and he's been talking. I've an idea he knows more about the murder than he's told us so far. What next, Sergeant?"

"Don't lose him until I've got into touch with Mr. Burke," came back the sergeant's crisp reply.

CHAPTER SIXTEEN

A SHOT IN THE DARK

CURTIS BURKE BOOKED a room at "The Sickle." He felt that the time had come when he could not reasonably tax the welcome hospitality of Ian Grenville and his father for a period that might possibly prove indefinite. Besides, he had other less sentimental reasons for desiring to be a free-lance.

The landlord of the old-fashioned inn was lavish in his promises to make him as comfortable as possible, and Burke felt that the man would certainly be as good as his word.

He had driven down from London in a police car. The driver, Sergeant Forster, remained with Burke at "The Sickle," for he was now Burke's chief assistant, ready and willing to undertake whatever jobs were assigned to him.

The two men were seated together in the empty smoke-room, planning like seasoned generals the first part of the campaign.

"The whole case," Burke was saying, "turns on whether we can get Vance to talk. If he refuses—and he's stubborn enough for that—we've got a devil of a lot of work to put in. You see, Forster, he's not the type of man who's readily scared. He just goes on denying everything without giving a fellow a chance to trip him up on matters of detail. As you know, Forster, the man who just wags his head and keeps on saying 'I know nothing about it' is the most difficult of all because he doesn't get you anywhere."

"What about the girl, sir? Do you think she knows anything?" Forster felt that Burke was relying too much on one individual.

"Miss Vance is an exceedingly charming young lady," Burke commented. "Naturally she is on the side of her father. I'm not optimistic about getting any 'change' out of her. Then there's Delisle. I'm much more interested in Mr. Delisle now that I know he lost money in the Mexican oil affair. You know, Forster, I've not yet had the pleasure of interrogating him, and I've a fancy that he's going to tell us something of interest."

"Well, here's hoping for the best," smiled Sergeant Forster as he raised his foaming tankard.

It was by this eight o'clock in the evening and Burke did not want to delay the third interview with Vance longer than was absolutely necessary. So, accompanied by Sergeant Forster, the pair made their way towards Blacon Grange.

The night was dark and Burke had only a vague idea of the direction. At length, after skirmishing around for a while they came upon the wall that bounded one side of the Vance estate. It was a low wall reinforced by a briar hedge on the other side.

"If we could manage to scramble over here," Burke suggested, "it would save us a quarter of a mile round by road. You can see the lights of the house yonder."

"That should not be difficult, Mr. Burke," opined the Sergeant; "Here goes." Burke watched his bulky form drawn up to the top of the wall where it remained poised for a moment, then it disappeared. "Coast's clear, Mr. Burke," called the officer, "there's an easy way through the hedge. Might have been made for us."

A moment later the pair were crossing the damp meadow towards the avenue of trees that bordered the drive of Blacon Grange. Both were silent, but they had not gone many paces when there came the hissing "Ping!" of a bullet which passed them with only an inch or two to spare. Immediately the two detectives dropped flat to the ground. Neither moved. Each heard the other's deep and anxious breathing, for it is not a particularly comforting thing to know that somewhere in the deep black shadows of the night an assassin waits with poised rifle or revolver—waiting for a target.

"What do you make of that?" asked Forster.

"Too close for comfort," whispered Burke. "Seemed to come from the centre of the field, too. See anyone, Forster?"

Sergeant Forster raised himself cautiously on one elbow and gazed in the direction from which they assumed the shot had come. For a moment the sergeant's eyes were fixed on the gloom. Only the wind stirred the fringe of trees ahead of them.

"We'd better crawl the remainder of the way," Burke cautioned. "I'd like to bet we're a damn good target for anyone using night glasses."

"That was a close thing, sir," apostrophised Forster. "Have we anyone in mind?"

They had reached the shelter of the fringe of trees, but neither of them immediately assumed an upright position.

"I suppose there must be quite a number of people in the world who just hate us, Forster. You can't be in this line of business without making a few enemies. All the same, I wish I could be sure who was behind that shot," he added. "Still, here's the house."

A few minutes later they reached Blacon Grange and found John Vance and his daughter at home.

"I've taken the liberty of bringing a friend along with me, Mr. Vance," Burke explained as he introduced Sergeant Forster. "I hope you won't mind. You see, sir, we may be staying in Blacon for some considerable time. How long we remain depends entirely upon yourself."

Pamela, who had arisen at their entrance and who had remained watching the formality of introduction, suddenly stepped forward. "Do I understand you to say, Mr. Burke, that you are staying here—here in this house?"

"That had not been my intention, Miss Vance. Sergeant Forster and myself are staying in the village, although I am afraid our inquiries will necessitate our being out here quite frequently. If we should chance to make nuisances of ourselves I hope you won't mind letting us know." There was more than a hint of veiled cynicism in Burke's tone that was by no means lost on Pamela, but Burke was already conscious that he was not going to get any information from the girl unless she wanted him to know it.

"But really, Mr. Burke," protested Vance quietly, "is it necessary always to descend on us at such a late hour of the night. But perhaps you didn't appreciate that it is closing up to eleven o'clock."

"As I have explained previously," Burke replied evenly, "no one regrets the necessity for this visit more than I do myself. Believe me, Mr. Vance, when I tell you it is not a pleasurable occupation to keep prying into people's private lives as I have occasionally to do. As to the lateness of the hour—we would probably have been here two hours sooner had not an attempt been made on our lives as we were walking across your park."

There was an uncomfortable silence in the room. Father and daughter stared at Burke with eyes wide with surprise.

"I don't quite understand, Mr. Burke," Vance faltered. "What happened—please tell me!"

"Someone having a little nocturnal shooting practice, I think," Burke smiled wryly. "There was only one shot, which seems to suggest that whoever fired it was firing at what he believed to be a definite target. When Forster and I flattened ourselves out on the grass the shooting ceased. Are you troubled with gunmen around Blacon, Mr. Vance?"

Pamela noted that her father's face had whitened and that his hands were gripping the back of one of the chairs tightly as he stood with it in front of him.

"But this is outrageous," cried Vance. "I'd no idea that this affair was actually—dangerous."

Burke swung around on him quickly: "What exactly do you mean by that?" he demanded, savagely.

The detective's tone was unexpected and Vance hesitated, bewildered.

"There's no need for insolence," broke in Pamela. "What Father means. . . ." But Burke interrupted her quickly.

"Your father is quite capable of speaking for himself," he told her. "Now, sir, you were saying. . . ."

John Vance passed a cold hand across his clammy brow. "I don't know what I'm saying," he answered absently. "It's like a nightmare—a terrible, hideous nightmare. Ever since you came down here, Mr. Burke, I've been haunted." Vance walked around the chair he had been gripping and sank into it with a gesture of sheer exhaustion.

"Why should you be haunted?" persisted Burke relentlessly.

"I'm haunted by ideas," Vance explained slowly. "It has been obvious to me ever since you first came down here and made certain suggestions about the murder of Martin Stone that you believe I *know* something about Stone that will lead you to his murderer. The insidious method of suggestion which you have employed has borne fruit. It has slowly eaten its way like rust into my mind, and I am beginning to persuade myself that I *do* know something."

Pamela sprang forward and fell on her knees beside her father's chair.

"Stop, Daddy! Stop!" she cried. "You mustn't speak like that. You don't know anything. How could you?"

Burke once again intervened. "I'm dreadfully sorry, Miss Vance, but I must protest against your interruptions. Your father is quite capable of telling me anything he desires me to know without any prompting from yourself."

"But can't you see he's ill! He wouldn't be talking as he is doing if he were normal. And it's all your fault," she accused. "You're putting ideas into his head and he's thinking over them so much that he's actually beginning to believe them."

Slowly and tenderly Burke lifted the girl to her feet. "I am more sorry than you realise, Miss Vance," he told her, looking her full in the eyes. "But you know as well as I do that from the first moment I set foot in this house I have been told nothing but lies. I am convinced your father has not told me the truth. Whether you know the truth or not I am not in a position to know. But one thing is certain: I am not leaving Blacon until I know the truth. That shot in the dark out there tonight has convinced me that here—here in this house lies the clue to the death of Martin Stone."

A movement beside him caused Burke to glance around. It was Forster, who had been standing by the fireside watching Vance seated there with eyes closed. At the inspector's last words he saw the man slump forward and jumped to his assistance.

"It's quite all right, Miss Vance," Burke assured the girl. "Nothing more than a simple faint."

Forster fetched the manservant, Birtles, with some brandy, and a few moments later John Vance opened his startled eyes, but when he spoke there was a thin smile on his bloodless lips.

"That was silly of me," he said quietly. "I suppose it's the result of getting all 'worked up' inside."

Birtles withdrew, but Forster, who had been eyeing the butler keenly during the time he had been in the room, stepped out after him into the hall.

The two men faced each other, eyes unflinching.

"How long have you been calling yourself Birtles?" Forster demanded.

Not so much as a flicker disturbed Mr. Birtles' eyelids. "I'm afraid I don't understand you, sir."

"Oh, yes, you do! How about projecting that mind of yours back for, shall we say, twelve years? . . . standing in the dock at the Manchester assizes. Your name wasn't Birtles then, was it? Wasn't it James Clinton, and wasn't the charge one of forgery?"

"You must be mistaken, sir," answered the butler without a tremor. "I have never been to Manchester."

"Bluff," snapped Forster. "But it won't do, Clinton. I know you. I never forget a face. You got three years, didn't you?"

Birtles shook his head. "I repeat, sir, that you are mistaken. Twelve years ago I was in South Africa."

Then Forster suddenly changed his front.

"Been out walking tonight, Birtles?"

"No, sir."

"There's mud on your boots—fresh mud by the looks of it."
Forster suddenly stooped and picked something from the welt of the
man's right boot. "And a little blade of grass, Birtles. We'll have to
have a chat about this. It's damp, and yet you tell me you haven't
been out walking in the park tonight. Now, that's what I call odd.
Don't you? Or perhaps you're growing grass in the butler's pantry.
Yes, we'll certainly have to have a little chat about old times and
present ones, Birtles."

CHAPTER SEVENTEEN

"I WANT THE TRUTH"

WHEN SERGEANT FORSTER went back to the lounge where Burke was continuing his investigation, he found that the atmosphere of the room, if it had been electric before, was now highly inflammable. Vance had recovered. He was sitting in the same chair. In another quite close to him sat Pamela, a strained look on her white face.

"I want the truth," Burke was saying. "The last time I had occasion to ask you a few questions you distinctly told me the weapon rack in the hall was incomplete. Why did you lie to me?"

Father and daughter exchanged quick, significant glances.

"You won't scare me into any admission, Burke." Vance's voice sounded truculent. "What I told you before was the truth."

Burke looked at the pair with a gesture of desperation.

"Look here," he went on, "I really don't understand why two such highly intelligent people will persist in endeavouring to sidetrack the truth. You know you are lying, Mr. Vance, so why not say that you had no idea until you read about the murder that someone had stolen a weapon from your collection? That's all I want to know. Do you still maintain that the weapon is missing?"

Neither spoke. Then Pamela said: "Mr. Burke, would you mind very much if Daddy and I spent a few minutes together? I want to talk to him—alone."

"I've no objection at all, Miss Vance. I'll agree to anything if only it will end this ridiculous situation."

"Thank you."

Burke and Forster stepped out into the hall.

Left alone, Pamela turned to her father. "What are we going to do?"

"We agreed to say nothing," answered her father. "Are you weakening?"

"No!" exclaimed the girl emphatically. "But I'm beginning to feel afraid. I feel that sooner or later that man will find— everything."

"Until he does," declared Vance, "I am saying nothing."

"Well?" asked Burke as Pamela summoned them back to the room. "I hope that as a result of the family conference we are going to be sensible."

"We have considered the matter," intimated Vance, "and we have come to the conclusion that there is a great deal of wisdom in the old tag, 'Least said, soonest mended.' "

"Which means that I can expect no help from either of you?"

John Vance looked pained. He had always prided himself on his good citizenship, but now he was conscious that he was being definitely antisocial. He realised his own innocence, but could do nothing to establish it. If all the facts were known—and Burke would certainly want to know every iota if he discovered the truth about that letter and the journey to London to meet Stone—the circumstantial evidence against him would be so weighty that he could not see that there would be any hope for him at a trial.

Receiving no reply, Burke went on: "Well, Mr. Vance, much as I regret it, I have with me authority not only to question members of your staff here, but also a warrant to search the premises, should I consider such a course necessary. By the way, have you any firearms in the house?"

"Only an old-fashioned German revolver. It's in the drawer in my room. Would you like to see it?"

"I suppose it wasn't fired tonight by any chance?" asked Burke.

"Not to my knowledge. But I see what you are driving at. I think you said someone fired at you as you were coming through the park. Well, I can tell you quite definitely it was not I. Neither Pamela nor myself have left the house all the evening."

"I'll have a look at the revolver before I leave," Burke told him. "Now, about Tuesday. Can you tell me what you were doing on that day?"

"Certainly," said Vance. "I remained here until late in the afternoon. Then I took the car and went over to Gloucester. I felt at a loose end, and on such occasions I like nothing better than driving slowly around the byroads of the two counties. You won't find finer scenery anywhere, Mr. Burke. It is the heart of England—a most fascinating pursuit, discovering one's own country. It is so soothing, too."

"And what time did you return?"

"Pamela can vouch for that. It would be about half-past eleven as near as I can tell you."

"Do you seriously suggest to me that for approximately seven hours you did nothing but drive around lanes—even in the dark! A handicap to admiring rural England, don't you think, Mr. Vance?"

"Moonlight can be as beautiful as day. It was, you remember, a clear night and the stars were brilliant."

Burke turned away with a gesture of despair.

"And where was Miss Pamela?" he asked suddenly.

"I went with Mr. Delisle to Hereford to meet some friends of his who were motoring through to Holyhead. We accompanied them in Mr. Delisle's car as far as Shrewsbury, where we stayed for tea and then returned. Daddy came in about eleven-thirty. Mr. Delisle was here with me. He can vouch for what I am saying."

"That's something," grumbled Burke. "But I take it," he went on, turning to Vance, "that your story about driving around country lanes rests entirely on your own unsupported evidence?"

"That is so, Mr. Burke. Somehow, one usually potters about lanes alone."

"You didn't stop anywhere for tea?"

Vance replied in the negative.

"Excuse, me, sir," broke in Forster, "but how long has the man Birtles been in your employment?"

Vance pondered the question for a moment. "For the past seven years, as nearly as I can remember."

"Do you know anything about him prior to his coming here?"

"I'm afraid not—except his own word. He told me he had recently returned from South Africa. But what, may I ask, is the object of this questioning?"

"Just an idea that occurred to me," answered the sergeant.

Next morning Burke and Forster were astir early and long before the normal hour for breakfast they had left "The Sickle" and made their entrance into the parkland of Blacon Grange, in the same fashion as they had adopted on the previous night.

Coming to the spot where they had been crouching from the assassin, both men made a careful search of the ground in the direction from which they imagined the bullet had been fired. It was Forster who first discovered the hollow in the meadow and beckoned to Burke.

"Here we are," he said jubilantly. "You can just make out the impression in the turf where he was lying"—indicating a disturbance of the grass and the two small indentations made by the toes of someone's boots.

"Interesting, but not very helpful," was Burke's comment, as he wheeled around in a circle, looking for footprints in the soft meadowland. But though both of them searched diligently they found nothing which would give them any indication of the direction the gunman had taken.

Next a search was made for the bullet. This was not so difficult because, knowing the spot from which it had been fired, calculations could be made as to the extent of its range. Taking a line at right-angles from the spot in the hollow directly over the place where they had dropped to the grass, the two men moved simultaneously towards the boundary wall beyond the hedge. A careful search of the wall showed that the bullet's trajectory must have been low—necessarily from the crest of the hollow—for a recently made chipping of the stone could mean nothing else but that the bullet had been deflected. A little way to the right Forster whistled softly to Burke, who, coming up to his assistant, found him pointing to the bole of an elm which emerged immediately behind the wall. About seven feet from the ground they saw the track of the bullet.

It was embedded a little way in the corrugated bark, and Forster had no difficulty in extracting it with his pocket-knife and laying it on the palm of Burke's hand.

Burke turned it over and grunted.

"Hm! A 7.65 mm. Browning," he diagnosed. "Well, let's get back for breakfast."

After the meal Burke made inquiries of Sergeant Mulliver regarding the location of the cottage where Delisle was staying, and they were fortunate in finding that gentleman at home. He greeted them affably and cheerfully.

"Come inside, gentlemen. I'm not a particularly early riser this morning. I hope you'll excuse my dressing-gown."

"Sorry to trouble you, Mr. Delisle, but I fancy you know why I have called."

"Not at all, Inspector."

"Then I'll tell you. You are aware, no doubt, that we are investigating the murder of a man named Stone, whose death occurred under mysterious circumstances last Tuesday. Now, in examining the dead man's papers I discovered that Mr. Rodney Delisle lost a considerable amount of money in a financial project sponsored by Stone and I was thinking. . . ."

Delisle broke in on the detective's narrative.

"That Rodney Delisle was so sore about that loss that he decided to murder the fellow, is that it?" he asked.

"Precisely," said Burke.

"I should hate to disillusion you, Mr. Burke, but you're wrong. Rodney Delisle could not possibly have done it."

Burke looked searchingly at the man's face. It was an enigma.

"I am aware that you have a perfectly good alibi," he said. "Miss Vance can corroborate your movements on Tuesday."

"It's not that," exclaimed Delisle. "The reason why Rodney Delisle could not have committed the murder is because he is dead."

"Dead?" Consternation came into Burke's eyes. "How can that be? Aren't you Rodney Delisle?"

It was evident that the situation was highly amusing to the man in the dressing-gown.

"It simply means that the Rodney Delisle mentioned in the list of subscribers to that Mexican oil ramp was my father. He died eighteen months ago."

Light dawned in Burke's mind.

"He lost heavily, I understand."

"Yes," answered Delisle simply, "he did. Fifteen thousand pounds."

Burke grimaced. "As much as that?"

Delisle nodded.

"Was your father acquainted with oil prospects in Mexico that would induce him to invest such an amount?" was the detective's next question.

"He'd been out there years ago—before I was born."

"That would account for it," admitted Burke. "And I suppose, too, that the estate you inherited, Mr. Delisle, would be impoverished to the amount of your father's losses?"

"Naturally."

"Then you had every reason to be sore on your own account?"

"If I possessed a vindictive nature I suppose I might," Delisle admitted thoughtfully. "But I don't see how Stone's death was going to do me any good."

"I believe you are described as being a gentleman of private means, Mr. Delisle?"

Delisle shrugged his shoulders and smiled.

"They are so private, Inspector, that I have the utmost difficulty in getting to know them!"

Burke laughed. Delisle wasn't, after all, such a bad sort of fellow, he considered. His father had probably, despite the oil crash, managed to leave him a sufficiency.

"Well, thank you for seeing us, Mr. Delisle. Oh, by the way," asked Burke as an afterthought, "have you by any chance a Browning revolver in your possession?"

Delisle shook his head. "Nothing whatever like that, Mr. Burke. To tell you the truth, I'm scared of anything that shoots."

Forster had meanwhile been a silent witness to the interrogation. He sat on the latticed window-sill with half-closed eyes.

Down the lane that led them to the main road Forster said: "What did you make of that bird, Chief?"

"I haven't quite made up my mind," Burke admitted. "But you might send through to headquarters and get them to check up on Rodney Delisle senior."

"You know, Chief," went on Forster in that same matter-of-fact tone he invariably used, "I don't know how you felt about it, but I got the impression that all the time we were talking to that guy we weren't exactly alone."

Burke halted suddenly.

"What do you mean?"

"It's just an impression I got," answered Forster doggedly.

"Of course, there may have been someone in the house—I think I remember Mulliver saying something about a chauffeur-gardener."

"If that's true, sir, all that talk about his infinitesimal income was all ballyhoo. Men-servants are usually costly pieces of work these days. D'you mind if I run back and take a look?"

"Not so long as you do it discreetly."

When the police officers had taken their leave Rodney Delisle took a large silk handkerchief from the pocket of his dressing-gown and mopped his forehead. As he did so a door beside the staircase opened cautiously.

"That you, Grainger?" he called.

"Have they gone?" asked the man who emerged from the inner room.

Delisle nodded.

"Pour me a spot of brandy," commanded Delisle.

Grainger crossed to the cupboard, produced a decanter, and Delisle noted that he set two glasses on the table.

"Are we expecting a visitor?" he asked cynically.

"The other's for me, Guv'nor. If Forster'd seen me, he might have taken a greater interest in you. I think I've earned this drink."

"Well, you've only got yourself to blame. If you'd done as I told you last night Forster wouldn't have paid us a visit this morning."

With which enigmatic observation Delisle went upstairs to complete his toilet, leaving Grainger to help himself to the brandy.

"I'm clearing out this afternoon, boss," came Grainger's voice. "This quiet little burg's got quite unhealthy all of a sudden."

"I think I'll come with you for a day or two," came back Delisle's voice. "In any event, it's getting near the London season."

Sergeant Forster caught up Burke at the junction of the lane with the main road.

"Two gentlemen will be leaving for London this afternoon," he informed the inspector.

"Two?" queried Burke, puzzled.

"Mr. Delisle and his pal, Scully Grainger. You know, Chief, this rural retreat strikes me as being a funny sort of place—sort of convalescent centre for Dartmoor. First Clinton turns up in the guise of Birtles, the Vance butler, and now if I don't light on Scully Grainger, who went down for a two-year stretch five years ago. This case isn't as simple as I thought it was."

"Simple?" echoed Burke. "I like that, Forster, but what a Job's comforter you are, to be sure."

CHAPTER EIGHTEEN

AFTER CHURCH

ON SUNDAY MORNING Pamela Vance went to church as usual. She had not seen Delisle since Friday afternoon, when he had revealed himself to her as a man who would stick at nothing to gain his desires. And she had been in love with him! That was the amazing thing. The experience had shattered her faith in human nature. There were times when she felt she could scarcely trust herself. Pamela admitted to herself that Delisle had extracted her promise to marry him under a threat, and that was something she would never forget.

During the service she pondered the situation. It seemed incredible that she and her father could have become so deeply implicated in a crime in which they were completely disinterested. In some obscure way they had become pawns; her father more particularly than herself. Her faith in human justice had been shaken, too. Only too well she realised that to tell the truth would be fatal, and yet all day she had been wondering whether it might not be the best course after all. To do so would, perhaps, release her from her hateful and now repugnant promise to Rodney Delisle. But that telling of the truth was not for her. Her father must decide on that.

On the far side of the church she caught a glimpse of Ian Grenville, and she remembered she had been pretty beastly to him of late and he had never deserved it. Now, in the moment of her trial, she felt that she wanted someone in whom she could confide. The women in Blacon were for the most part too divided in age from her to be considered companionable, but even if they had been of her own generation her present trouble was something which could not somehow be entrusted to a woman's confidence. Yet how could she speak of it to Ian, who was a friend of Inspector Burke?

At the end of the service she found Ian awaiting her beside the old-fashioned bower-gate. He raised his hat and smiled a greeting.

"I want you to walk back home with me, Ian," said Pamela quietly, "that is if you have the time," she added.

"You know jolly well I would make time for that," he told her eagerly. "I'm awfully sorry about all this wretched business, Pamela. I suppose old Curty has been worrying you?"

She nodded. "I've no quarrel with Mr. Burke, Ian. I realise he has his duty to perform, and even if he does happen to be hopelessly mistaken we can do nothing to prevent his asking questions and prowling around. Did you hear that someone tried to kill him the other night—a shot fired from the grounds? Daddy's very worried about it."

Ian had not heard. In fact, he had not set eyes on Curtis Burke since the latter's return to Blacon, although he had heard that Burke and an assistant had taken rooms at "The Sickle."

"By Jove!" he exclaimed, "things must be getting warm. Has he any idea who could have tried to kill him?"

"I gather that he hasn't," Pamela told him, "although we've been having a respite from Mr. Burke's personal attentions for a few hours. The servants haven't been quite so lucky. They've been pestered with questions so often that their efficiency in the house is being seriously affected."

"But what have the servants got to do with it," asked Ian, puzzled.

"As far as I can understand it, Mr. Burke has some crazy idea that the man Stone was killed with a dagger which was stolen from Daddy's collection in the hall."

They had reached the point where the main road branched sharply to the right and was intersected by a small road which ran in the direction of Blacon Grange.

"That's interesting," said Ian. "I wonder what gave him that idea?"

Pamela confessed that she had not the remotest notion. She was wanting desperately to tell Ian all about it and was wondering whether she dared so much as hint at it. Then an idea came into her head and she said: "I suppose you have heard that I am engaged to be married to Rodney Delisle?"

Ian had experienced many shocks in his life, but none which bowled him over so completely as this one. She had asked him to walk with her just for this! And he had thought that he was getting on so well—that the little cloud of the past week or two was being dispersed and he was preparing to bask in the sun of her favour once more. But this! The bitterest chagrin overwhelmed the young man. If he had not heard it from the girl's own lips he would have refused to have believed it. He stopped suddenly and stood staring at her, stark unbelief in his blue eyes. And then he realised that there were tears—real tears running down Pamela's face, and that she was searching desperately in the pocket of her coat for a handkerchief.

"Why, Pamela, you're crying," he managed to say. "I always thought engaged girls were happy."

For the life of him Ian Grenville could not think of anything better to say. He was still suffering from the shock her words had given him, and in moments of shock one is apt to utter trivial banalities.

"I suppose I should be happy," she said, "but I'm not, Ian—I'm dreadfully unhappy. That's why I wanted you to walk home with me. I wanted to tell you to tell you everything."

They passed together through the ornamental iron gateway of Blacon Grange and made their way slowly towards the house. Then the girl paused.

"Let's go through the rose-garden," she suggested. "No one will disturb us in the summer-house."

Ian readily consented. It was obvious to him that Pamela was in the midst of serious trouble, and the way she was talking about her engagement to Delisle seemed to suggest that in some way he could not as yet fathom that trouble was bound up with Delisle.

They reached the summer-house and unlocked the door. It was a substantially built rustic structure with a window at either side—more in fact in the nature of a garden pavilion than anything else. Pamela sat down on one of the red-cushioned seats.

"What I am going to tell you, you know," she began, "is entirely between our two selves. You must not breathe a word about it—not even to your friend Burke. You must promise me that. I know I am asking a great deal of you, Ian, but when I have told you I do believe that you'll understand."

"You know very well that I'll do anything to help you, Pamela," he said in a low voice, with absolute sincerity.

Her eyes were dry again now, and she told him exactly what her father had told her. Pamela began from the beginning with the receipt of the letter from the unknown writer. When she had made up her mind to a course she did nothing by halves. If Ian was to understand and help her he must know every detail. Her quiet recital finished with the interview with Delisle and the threat he had made.

"The swine!" cried Ian, with blazing eyes. "I'd like to—"

Pamela held up a restraining hand.

"That won't help, Ian," she told him, still in that quiet, low-pitched voice in which she had been talking, "but you see how dreadfully important it all is in the light of what I've said."

Ian certainly realised that only too clearly. The case was even more complicated than Burke himself could have anticipated. To Grenville's mind it savoured of a deliberate plot to foist the responsibility of Stone's murder on to an innocent man; and oddly enough, for a man so astute in business as John Vance, Pamela's father had played right into these unknown people's hands.

"We'll leave Delisle out of this for a moment," said Ian, "and try to fathom the first part. We'll have to accept that letter for what it is worth. As far as I can see that letter was sent with the object that your father would not destroy it and that when the time came it could be used as damnable evidence against him, allied to the fact, of course, that it was his dagger that was found. Next we come to the telephone call. I suppose he is quite certain that Stone was actually the person speaking to him?"

"He says he would recognise Stone's voice anywhere—even over a telephone wire. I am convinced from what Daddy says that Stone did want to see him. What he wanted to see him about must now remain a mystery."

"It may have been that Stone himself had got wind of the plot against his life and wanted to consult your father. He would know him for an honest man and not a cut-throat," Ian suggested. "But whatever our theories may be concerning that, the fact remains that whoever it was killed Stone knew of that telephone message and staged Stone's murder to coincide with your father's visit to the office."

"That's what we both think," Pamela told him desperately. "But how can Daddy prove anything, especially as the dagger that was used did really belong to him?"

"I can appreciate that point and was coming to it. Of course, your father must have thought he was doing the right thing when he removed that dagger. I suppose if I'd been in his place I'd have acted in precisely the same way. Yet perhaps he should have summoned the police straight away. And yet I don't know. Things would have looked very sticky for him. Gosh! Whoever planted that on him knew how to stage things! What we've got to get at is who could have stolen that dagger and when it was removed. Something of a problem, I'll admit."

Pamela brightened suddenly. "I feel heaps better now that I've told you, Ian. Such a load has been taken off my mind. It's quite true, you know, that saying about a 'trouble shared is a trouble halved.' "

"Perhaps, too, it depends on the person it's shared with," suggested Ian in his usual diffident manner, "but you know you can certainly count on me to help you in any way possible," he assured her.

"But where are we going to begin?"

"With the dagger, of course," he replied. Yet there was a feeling in the young man's mind that it was not going to be quite so easy as it seemed.

"I suppose you've no idea how long it has been missing?" he followed up.

Pamela shook her head. "Daddy says he hasn't the remotest idea. You see, he had never missed it until Mr. Burke mentioned the matter—no—until—until—you know when," she broke off.

"I must certainly have a chin with Curty about the whole matter," Ian said with determination. "Of course, I won't say a word about what you've just told me." Then he remembered that there was another and equally distasteful side to this confidence . . . Pamela's engagement to that bounder Delisle. It revolted him to think that any man could be such a swine as to take advantage of a position like this to force a girl's hand, and what a threat he had used! Ian felt he could quite understand how Pamela had felt about it that afternoon. Delisle knew so well that John Vance did not want the police to know anything at all about the letter.

"What are you going to do about your engagement?" he asked hesitantly.

"What can I do?" The question was asked with an intonation of utter helplessness.

"You certainly can't go on with it," Ian told her. "My own opinion is that Delisle is a blackmailer. If he is you must go to the police."

For a moment she admired his enthusiasm. Then she said: "Aren't the police the very people we wish to avoid? Everything would come out."

"I'm beginning to wonder if it wouldn't all be for the best," he said slowly. "It may be the one way of getting at the truth. Truth can't be hidden for ever."

Such words might have consoled her, but what she was dreading was that before the truth could come out the talons of the law would have gripped her father and held him prisoner for a horrible crime which he had never committed.

"I'll come along and see you tomorrow," Ian promised. "Try not to worry too much. I'll go along and see Burke this afternoon just to find out if he can or will tell me anything."

" 'Phone me if you have any news," she said after a wan good-bye, as she turned to go down the drive.

The man watched her disappear in the direction of the house. She had smiled at him—she had confided in him—and he—he felt curiously elated. In spite of her dreadful predicament, Ian Grenville felt almost light-headed with a deep-down warm happiness. She was certainly not going to marry Delisle.

If Pamela Vance married anyone at all that one would he Ian Grenville, because Ian Grenville himself had decided that!

CHAPTER NINETEEN

IAN "TAKES A RIDE"

CURTIS BURKE COMPLETED a full report for headquarters by five o'clock that same Sunday afternoon. None realised better than he that the report was manifestly unsatisfactory. It didn't lead anywhere. It stated merely that John Vance was not telling the truth; that the dagger which killed Martin Stone was doubtless the same that had once completed the collection of weapons in Blacon Grange.

Next there were the observations of Sergeant Forster relative to the presumed identity of Birtles, John Vance's butler, and the chauffeur-gardener who was employed by Rodney Delisle. Burke was still convinced that the murder was the result of the oil swindle, but as to who had actually done the deed and for precisely what objective except that of sheer revenge he was none the nearer. He ruled out altogether the possibility of Colonel Sir John Grenville being implicated. Sir John had not left Blacon for the past three years—could not, indeed, because of his disability. Rodney Delisle had said that he would have no motive; that it was his father who had directly suffered.

Place, too, was found in the report of the attempt which had been made on the lives of himself and Sergeant Forster. The inquiry had yielded nothing. In short, the case was as unsatisfactory a one as Burke had ever handled.

Forster was disconsolate. He had believed from what he had overheard the previous morning that both Delisle and his man Grainger would be quitting that afternoon, but from his own observation nothing of the kind had occurred. He urgently wanted to go and have a word with friend Grainger, but Burke had forbidden such a course, on the ground that if there was anything behind Delisle at all—and he himself was inclined to believe that there was not—he had no intention of startling the coterie by precipitate action. He did not wish to expose more cards in his hand that need be at the moment. Forster knew just where and when he could get

Grainger when he wanted him, while it was exceedingly unlikely that Delisle himself, with Pamela Vance so near him, would skip.

The landlord knocked on the private door and mentioned that Mr. Grenville was inquiring for Mr. Burke.

"Well, my lad, and where have you been hiding yourself these past few days?" greeted Burke with a cheerfulness that belied his feelings.

"Just working hard," returned Grenville, taking the proffered seat.

"Forster, this is Ian Grenville, an old college pal of mine," Burke introduced the pair.

"Good afternoon, sir," said Forster. "Always pleased to meet any friends of Inspector Burke," and with that he sat clown in his chair by the window and became automatically immersed in his Sunday newspaper.

"Anything to report, old boy?" asked Burke.

"I have and I haven't."

"That's helpful. What about starting on the news that you haven't?"

"Not on your life, Curty. But I can tell you something you don't know. Miss Vance is engaged to be married to Delisle. How's that for a sensation?"

Burke elevated his eyebrows. "You don't say! But isn't that rather distressing to a certain young man of my acquaintance?"

"Oddly enough, it isn't," Grenville told him, "because the promise was given under a threat, and it was to me that Pamela came to tell the news."

"Now that does sound interesting. I gather that the young lady in question had been so long in making up her mind that Delisle began to put the screw on. Well, there's nothing much in that, Ian. Many a man has done the same. It does bring the reluctant damsel to the sticking point. Some threaten to destroy themselves. They talk moodily about the 'river' and all that sort of rot. It's a form of conceit I've never been able to understand. Is that all?"

"I suppose you find it humorous, Curty," said Ian seriously. "But there's more to it than you think. The fellow's an out-and-out rotter, that's what he is."

Burke had grown interested beneath his veneer of joviality. The news was strange, in view of the troubled state of the minds at Blacon Grange, and Burke was already beginning to wonder whether the case he had in hand had not something to do with this suddenly announced engagement.

"And what is this dire threat," he asked pleasantly. "Suicide's about the worst I can think of in the circumstances."

"I can't tell you," replied Ian. "I was told it in confidence by the lady concerned. It's no use your asking me or trying to bully it out of me. I've promised not to say anything."

"Something to do with Stone's murder?" The words came calmly and quietly, as though in the ordinary course of friendly conversation.

"I'm not rising to that bait, old chap," said Ian with a bitter laugh. "I merely thought you'd be interested in my news."

"I'm positively thrilled, old thing, especially as you appear confident that 'the marriage will not take place.' "

"I never said any such thing," Ian protested hotly.

"Not in so many words," smiled Burke, "but there is hope in your face and a certain light in your eye. . . !"

Ian changed the subject abruptly.

"How's the case going? Any more suspects?" he asked.

"I had your venerable father on my list a day or two ago."

"Father! That's rich! Are you going through all the names in Blacon and popping them down? What's the old man supposed to have done?"

"Nothing. Nothing at all! I've struck him off and put your name down in his place."

"My name! Is it the privilege of friendship with the high and mighty of Scotland Yard to be tagged on to every list of suspects for every blessed crime they investigate? Really, Curty, you ought to take something for it—or see someone. There's a good man in Harley Street named Dancing or something like that. I'm told lots of detectives go to him for a mental tonic."

But Burke was serious.

"Why didn't you tell me that your father lost some money in that oil swindle I was telling you about in which Stone was interested?"

"Really, Curty—but this is news to me. I'd no idea." The young man was obviously taken aback. "I'd heard the pater had dropped a packet on the market a few years ago, but I never knew until this minute that it was in Mexican oil. The old man's pretty close on his business flutters . . . thinks he's a hell of a fine fellow on gilt-edges and things like that. But why me?"

"Of course, if you didn't know that rather alters the situation, doesn't it?" said Burke with mock concern. "Forster," he called, "take Mr. Ian Grenville's name off the black list, will you?"

"Right, sir," came back the voice from behind the newspaper.

"Thanks. And now that I'm no longer under suspicion I suppose I may be admitted into the secret counsels of Scotland Yard," smiled Ian. "How goes it, Curty?"

But Burke shook his head. "There's nothing doing, old fellow. I'm no nearer today that I was when I first came down. Except," he added, "that I am convinced that Vance and his daughter are not playing the game with me."

"What makes you think that?"

"They're both as dumb as oysters, that's why."

"Has it ever occurred to you that perhaps they have a very good reason for their silence?" asked Ian.

"That thought has crossed my mind, and I can see now that you, too, have been admitted to the Ancient Order of Clams. Come along, old boy, and spill the beans. What did really happen last Tuesday night when Vance was supposed to be out stargazing?"

"I'm sorry," said Ian earnestly, "but I can't tell you."

"That means that you won't!"

"All right, if you put it like that."

"Won't you tell me, not even if I give you my solemn promise that no harm shall come to either father or daughter?" Burke persisted.

Ian began to falter. If Burke gave such a promise it meant that he would keep it absolutely. Would that mean that he would not be breaking faith with Pamela? Burke noticed his hesitation and followed up with: "Vance cannot suffer if he is innocent of this crime. I'll give you my word that no annoyance or trouble shall come to him through what you may tell me."

"I'll tell you what I'll do," said Ian. "I'll think it over. Give me until ten o'clock tomorrow morning. We'll make the appointment here. How will that do?"

"Suits me," Burke agreed in a satisfied tone.

The sun was shining—a pale daffodil sun—as Ian Grenville made his way homewards. His promise to Burke needed a good deal of thinking over, and he wondered whether or not he ought to acquaint Pamela of his interview with the detective. By the time he reached home he had decided against the adoption of such a course. Any action he might take must be on his own initiative.

But he was not solely concerned with this predicament between friendship of long standing on the one hand and love and a promise on the other. He was thinking of Delisle, and thought of that gentleman, combined with his own justifiable prejudice against the man, caused him suddenly to realise that Delisle might easily assume a much greater significance in this drama than any of them had so far realised.

In the first place, what did anyone know of Delisle beyond the fact that he was reputed to be quite wealthy and that he had no visible means of support. Ian thought with some bitterness of the hours Delisle had been free to spend with Pamela while he himself had to work to find his daily bread. What if, for some reason, Delisle himself had some perfectly good reason for killing this Martin Stone, who somehow had become inextricably mixed up with various members of the little Blacon community. He had an alibi, of course, but that might mean nothing at all. One could instigate a murder, even if one was far away when the actual blow was struck. Pamela had been perplexed to know how and by whom the dagger had been removed. What more reasonable assumption than that it had been taken by Delisle himself. For months he had had almost free entry to Blacon Grange as a result of his friendship with Pamela.

The thought obsessed him. The more he turned it over in his mind, the more real did the possibility become. Ian hated Delisle. He believed him capable of anything—even of murder . . . yet Burke—Burke of all people, thought Ian, did not appear to suspect Delisle at all.

After tea the idea had gripped him so strongly that he decided to do a little detecting on his own. He knew Delisle's cottage quite well, and he also knew that there were means of reaching the garden without being seen from either the house or the road. The Grenvilles' own lands adjoined an estate which was adjacent, and he knew that his presence there, even on a Sunday evening, would arouse no comment.

He crossed two fields and moved cautiously in the shelter of a high hedge until he was close to the garden at the rear of Virginian Cottage. A moment later he was actually in the garden. The daylight was fading quickly and he hugged the shadows until he was quite close to the house. It was then that he noticed Delisle's coupé standing out in the lane with the engine ticking over rhythmically. Grenville edged a little nearer, squeezing himself against the angle of the cottage near the front. Then he heard Delisle's voice: "Where the devil are you, Grainger? We don't want to be driving all night."

"I'm coming," answered the man.

Grenville did not wait to hear more. Creeping in the shadow of the hedge he made his way to the lane where the car was standing, There was no luggage in the closed occasional seat at the back and none in front. Cautiously he looked over the hedge to see if anyone stood ready in the cottage porch. As he did so the man Grainger came out. All he carried was a rug and an overcoat. This decided Grenville. At all costs he was determined to discover where Delisle was going, and before Grainger came out into the lane the young man had opened the seat at the back scrambled inside and closed the lid. He was taking a chance: he knew that, but he felt it was worth the risk.

He heard Delisle say something to Grainger, and then the door in front slammed. The next moment the car slid away down the lane towards the main road.

After they had been going for some minutes Grenville considered it expedient to raise the lid of his hiding-place and ascertain which direction they were taking. This operation needed only an inch or two, for the knew the road particularly well. The car was heading eastwards to Gloucester, and thence probably to London.

It was the most uncomfortable journey Grenville ever remembered. Crouching on the floor of the occasional seat he was at the mercy of the car's undeniable high speed. Added to this, the compartment was airless, so, to remedy this defect and make the remainder of the journey a little more pleasant, Grenville jacked up the lid an inch or two with a loose spanner which he had discovered in the most unpleasant manner possible by kneeling on it.

The night became as black as ink, but whoever was driving paid little heed to the darkness. The car must, according to the young man's estimate of speed, have been travelling close to the mile a minute figure. The hours went by, but no stop was made. The towns through which they passed were quite big places. Grenville looked at his watch. The luminous dial showed him that they had been travelling for five hours, and he was stiff with cramp. If they were heading for London—as indeed they must be—he would not have much longer to wait.

He made his plans carefully. As there was no luggage in the compartment, the chances of his discovery were negligible, and he intended that as soon as the car finally pulled up he would wait until its occupants had alighted and gone into the house or hotel or wherever it was they were staying, and then he could emerge. What happened after that he must allow circumstances to decide. At all costs, however, he must send a telegram to Blacon, informing his father of his sudden call to London.

A sudden squealing of brakes warned him that the car was slowing down, and he braced himself for the next part of the ordeal.

For the past few miles he had been judiciously changing his position in an effort to unloose stiff limbs.

The car stopped, and he heard the engine being switched off.

The door in front opened, closed again and then—silence.

Now was his opportunity. Carefully he raised the lid a few inches and glanced through the aperture. The car was drawn up before what appeared to be a large house, and the door of the house was closed.

Pushing the lid up to its fullest extent and snapping the bracing pieces into position, Grenville clambered out and filled his lungs with the cool night air. Having closed the lid again he took further stock of his surroundings. The house was detached and was approached from the road by a short length of drive. A light shone in one of the upper rooms.

The first thing, he told himself, was to find out, if he could, what was happening—why, in fact, it had been necessary for Delisle and his man-servant to be in such a desperate hurry to reach London by midnight.

Grenville made his way round to the back of the house. The way was easy. It was an old house—probably Georgian. The cellar windows were barred, but he found one window without such protection, and fortunately it was open. Slowly he pushed it wider. It was of the sash-cord variety, and he was afraid of its making a warning noise. At last he managed to open it sufficiently for him to push his stiff legs over the sill and slowly he lowered himself to the stone floor.

Not having a torch, he had to resort to matches. In the light of one of these he saw that he was in a small pantry with bare shelves and a closed door facing him. He crossed to the door and tried the handle. It was not locked. Opening it a crack, he listened. No sounds came to his ears. Emboldened, he passed out into a narrow passage and found a flight of stone steps on his left. Up the steps he crawled, feeling his way with his fingers against their smooth surfaces. At the top he found a second door. This, too, yielded to his attentions. Now he found himself in what appeared to be the hall. An incandescent gas mantle provided some slight illumination and cast eerie yellow shadows beneath and above it.

He had noticed from the front that a light was burning behind a holland blind on the first floor. This, he decided, was his next objective.

The stairs creaked ominously, and he heard his heart beating with fear as he ascended, pausing at each step to listen for any warning sound from above.

Halting to take his bearings, he saw that a light showed dully beneath one of the doors, and Grenville crept forward on tip-toe to listen. With his ear pressed close to the panel, he heard men's voices, at first a confused monotone and then one voice was raised above the others. He recognised it instantly. It was Delisle's voice, and it said: "I've told you definitely that you'll have to wait for the money. You ought to know by this that things are not managed as quickly as all that. The police are still busy at Blacon. I hadn't anticipated that quite so soon. Still, things are moving quite nicely. I should say that in a day or two the old fool will be arrested. When that happens you can leave it to me to deal with the girl. I'm almost sure to get something on account. She'll do anything for him."

Grenville stiffened as he heard Delisle's words. What they meant he hadn't a shred of an idea, except that Delisle expected Vance to be arrested.

It was then that the unexpected happened. The front door opened and closed again, and Grenville heard a heavy tread ascending the stairs. Quickly he moved back into the shadows opposite the door. There was no time to seek refuge in any of the rooms which presumably led off the landing. The laboured breathing came closer. Then a light flashed out—the light from an electric torch. The man who held it gave vent to a fierce exclamation and flung himself on Grenville before the young man had time to act.

The confusion on the landing attracted the attention of those inside the room. The door opened and three men emerged quickly.

"What's all this," he heard Delisle's wavering voice.

Grenville felt himself being dragged to his feet, powerless in the man's grasp.

"Looks like someone listening in," muttered the newcomer. "Friend of yours, Mr. Delisle?" apparently noticing the look of surprise on the other's face.

"We have met before, I think," smiled Delisle, "and it looks as if we are going to see quite a lot of each other in the near future."

Grenville was hustled into the room and confronted by five burly-looking men.

"Who is he?" demanded one of them truculently.

"You heard me say he was a friend of mine," snapped Delisle petulantly. "You can leave him to me," he added on a note of menace and with a look on his face which Grenville interpreted as meaning that the enjoyment of this unexpected encounter would be all on one side.

CHAPTER TWENTY

WHO IS BIRTLES?

INSPECTOR CURTIS BURKE looked at the watch on his wrist and compared it frowningly with the clock on the mantel.

"Ten-fifteen," he grumbled. "Our young friend appears to have changed his mind."

"You expected him to come?" inquired Sergeant Forster, in a non-committal tone.

Burke nodded. "Yes," he admitted. "I thought he would have come through."

At that moment came a knock at the door of the room and in response to Burke's "Come in," the landlord entered.

"You're wanted on the telephone, Mr. Burke."

The telephone was in the landlord's own room.

"That Mr. Burke?" inquired a man's voice from the other end. ,

"Inspector Burke speaking. Who are you?"

"This is Grenville, Mr. Burke. Can you tell me if anything's happened to my son? I understand he had a talk with you yesterday. Did he, or did he not?"

"He certainly did," Burke told Sir John. "In fact he arranged to meet me this morning at ten o'clock. I haven't clapped eyes on him since yesterday afternoon."

"I went to bed early last night," Sir John Grenville told him. "He hadn't come home then. I didn't think much about that. He's often late. But this morning when my housekeeper told me he'd not been to bed . . . well, Burke, what's to be done about it? Ian's not the sort of boy to hare off like this without a word."

Burke was silent for a moment. He was thinking quickly.

"I shouldn't worry, if I were you, Sir John. I'm sure Ian can very well look after himself. But if it will prove any comfort to you, I'll have inquiries made immediately. I'm quite sure, in my own mind, that nothing serious can have happened to him."

Burke hung up the receiver and stood for a moment contemplating it. Then he wheeled about and returned to the room where he had left Forster.

"Young Grenville's vanished," he announced, closing the door behind him. "Not been home last night . . . not seen since he left here yesterday by all accounts."

"What do you think, sir?" Forster looked apprehensively across at his chief. "Is it an accident, sir, or just sheer dirty work?"

"That's just what we've got to find out, Forster," said Burke grimly. "I can't help thinking that the young man's disappearance is due solely to the fact that he knows more than we do. He knew something when he was here yesterday, and I'll swear it was something mighty important to this case. Well, this is where you do a spot of work, Forster. Circulate this description to all stations and then follow up with routine inquiries in the immediate neighbourhood. I'm off up to the Grange. I wonder," he mused in conclusion, "how Miss Pamela will take the news?"

For the next moment or two Burke busied himself with giving Forster a meticulous description of Ian Grenville and, as a test of his observation, gave an even more minute description of the clothes that young man had been wearing when last the detective had seen him.

Leaving the sergeant to get along with his job, Burke made his way to Blacon Grange.

The first person he met—and singularly enough it was the first person he most particularly desired to meet—was Birtles. Burke did not share his colleague's pessimism about Birtles.

"Good morning, Birtles! No, not yet," as the butler moved away towards the lounge. "I want a word or two with you."

Birtles paused, mystified.

"I suppose, Birtles, you are aware of Sergeant Forster's suspicion about you? Tell me, is there any truth in what he suggests?"

Birtles looked intensely relieved. "None whatever, sir. Clinton Birtles is my half-brother, so to speak, sir. People used to make funny jokes about the similarity in our appearance. As I told Sergeant Forster, sir, I was in South Africa at the time my half-brother was sent down at Manchester."

"And you have not heard from him for . . . how long, Birtles?"

"Just after the Armistice, sir. We met in London. He was a 'con' man. He invited me to join the syndicate but I declined. Was it Mr. Vance you wanted to see, sir, or Miss Pamela?"

Burke could not help smiling. "I think you're positively priceless, Birtles. I think I'll see them both this morning."

No sooner was Burke ushered into the lounge than he once again sensed that strange atmosphere of tension and antagonism.

"Good morning," greeted the detective, bowing stiffly to father and daughter, who arose at his entry. "Once again I must express my sorrow at troubling you two good people again. I know well enough you consider me an infernal nuisance, but the fact is I've lost someone. I suppose you don't happen to have seen him, have you?"

"Seen whom?" asked Pamela, interested.

"Mr. Grenville—Mr. Ian Grenville."

Pamela's eyes opened wider. "Ian," she cried. "What do you mean, Mr. Burke, when you say you have 'lost' him?"

"That's just what I want to find out, Miss Pamela. I understand that yesterday morning you two had a good long talk together. What you talked about is your own affair and doesn't concern me in the slightest, but if I may be permitted to venture a guess, I rather fancy it concerned your reported engagement to Mr. Delisle and also the trouble we all find ourselves in. Now I put it to you, Miss Vance, that if you gave Mr. Grenville information which you have denied me, it is just possible that by so doing you have been the means of placing his life in very grave danger."

The girl was breathing heavily and her eyes strayed across to her father, who had reseated himself in his deeply-upholstered armchair listening quietly but intently to the dialogue.

"But I do not see how my conversation with Ian could have done any harm, Mr. Burke. It sounds incredible."

"Incredible or not, the fact remains that he's gone," Burke told her without sentiment. "He disappeared apparently last night. His father 'phoned me half an hour ago to say that his bed had not been slept in. In fact, he has vanished as quietly and as mysteriously as it is possible to imagine. And what is more we have not the smallest clue to his whereabouts."

"But why should they try to get Ian?" asked Pamela, a frightened look in her eyes mixing with the perplexity they already held. "He did not know anything until. . . ." The girl paused suddenly, realising that she had already said too much.

Burke fixed the girl with a steady stare as she halted. "So there was something to know, eh?"

Pamela crossed to where her father was sitting and seated herself on the broad arm of his chair.

"There was and still is, Mr. Burke," she replied, quietly. "But you haven't yet told me the reason for Ian's disappearance."

Burke dropped down on to the divan facing father and daughter.

"There are several reasons why he should disappear," he began, and there was no mistaking now the hard edge to his voice, "but I will deal with only one of them. Has it not occurred to you that whatever you told him yesterday has been the means, perhaps, of placing his life in danger?"

At his words Pamela strangled a cry and her father placed a supporting arm around her waist.

"Supposing, Miss Vance, that what you told him gave Grenville an idea. Suppose it suggested to him the identity of the person who killed Martin Stone, and further than that, the murderer himself, realising that Grenville knew, decided for the sake of his own safety to remove the young man as speedily as possible from a sphere of activity which might make him a source of danger?"

"I see what you mean," Pamela admitted in a quiet voice. "Everything does seem to be in an awful tangle. What are we to do about it, Mr. Burke?"

"The solution is a simple one. There is yet time for your father to tell me the whole truth about last Tuesday. I'm here now to hear all about it."

John Vance leaned forward in his chair. "I think you're right, Mr. Burke. I can see now that I've been a fool. Yes, I'm going to tell you . . . everything. But when you have heard it I am sure you will agree that my silence—our silence perhaps I should say—had at least the merit of good intention."

Burke heaved a sigh of relief. At long last he was going to get at the truth. He looked at the girl. She remained passive, apparently in agreement with her father's belated course of action.

Curtis Burke listened intently while John Vance told his story, and with the telling of it the Inspector's interest grew. Mentally he visualised each small incident and when the recital had ended Vance remarked: "So you see, Mr. Burke, what an awkward position I was in. I suppose my telling you does not alter the seriousness of the situation so far as I am concerned?"

Burke pondered the problem. It was certainly an amazing story . . . the neatest, compactest little plot he had ever encountered . . . a plot conceived by a master mind.

"I shall have to think things over carefully," Burke told them, "but I still think it would have been wiser to have been perfectly frank with me from the start. You see now I have the addition of Ian Grenville's disappearance, which, as I mentioned, I am convinced has some bearing on the plot underlying the story you have just told me. Now let us get down to facts. You will let me have the weapon, of course. That is vitally necessary." Vance nodded in complete agreement. "Now," proceeded the detective, "can you tell me anything more about this Mexican society? You see, Mr. Vance, whichever way we look at it we cannot altogether absolve Mexico, whether it be as regards oil or purification."

Vance explained in greater detail the facts about the society to which he had belonged.

"And you know no one today who was also a member of that society?"

"I have thought the matter over every day since receiving that letter, Mr. Burke, and I cannot recall anyone who might have returned to England."

"Yet someone must have the information," Burke insisted. "Someone must have knowledge of your connection with the movement. We have got to find out who that 'someone' is. Now, when you heard Stone's voice over the wire did it sound at all apprehensive?"

"I knew Stone well, Mr. Burke. At one time we were bosom friends, but during my final year in business we had a disagreement. I did not like some of the stocks he was handling and I made no bones about making known my disapproval."

"And you have not seen him since?"

"Never! I did not wish to see him and I am equally certain he had no desire to see me."

"The disagreement must have been a serious one!"

"We almost came to blows. Stone threatened to fling me out of his office."

"As bad as that? It occurs to me, Mr. Vance, that there's someone who appears to know a whole heap about you and your relations with Stone. You can't think who that can be?"

Vance shook his head. "I've been trying for a week," he groaned despairingly.

"And now I'd like to see the weapon," announced Burke in businesslike tones.

Together they ascended the staircase to Vance's bedroom.

Burke watched Vance cross the room to the bureau and take the weapon, still wrapped in the blood-stained handkerchief, from the back of the desk calendar and hand it to him.

Carefully the inspector unwrapped it until the dagger lay on the handkerchief. He was careful not to touch it with his naked fingers, and after a moment's silent scrutiny he wrapped it up again and placed it in his pocket.

"What is the next move, Mr. Burke?" asked Vance, in obvious relief that he could not conceal.

"I shall, of course, send this along to Scotland Yard," Burke told him. "I shall, too, be obliged to place all the details as I now know them before the commissioner, but if it is any comfort to you at all, I will say this: I believe you are innocent, Mr. Vance, and innocent men need have little fear. You have given me a great deal of important information and I shall act immediately. But there is one thing I want you to promise me, and that is you will divulge to no one the fact that you have told me what you have done. That is of paramount importance, especially if the case proves to be as I now visualise it for the moment. I want you to go about your life here at Blacon just as if you are still hugging your secret, for I believe there is someone who knows that secret as well as you do yourself. Sooner or later I am convinced that person will come out into the open and show his hand. Until then we have got to wait . . . to play the waiting game."

Vance gave the promise readily enough.

Down below in the hall they found Pamela awaiting them.

"What do you intend to do about Ian?" she asked Burke seriously.

He drew her aside and spoke quietly.

"You don't want any harm to come to Ian, do you, Miss Pamela?"

Slowly the warm colour flooded her face.

"I love him, Mr. Burke," she told him simply.

"And Delisle . . . you haven't told me about your engagement?" he prompted.

"I was intending to tell you, Mr. Burke. I told Ian yesterday."

Briefly she told him what had occurred and when she had finished there was a grim setting to his jaw.

"Just one word of warning to you, young lady," he said seriously. "You must on no account tell Delisle that I know anything about it or about what your father has told me, but any further suggestions he may make to you must be conveyed to me as quickly as possible."

The girl's eyes widened. "You don't mean. . . ."

"I don't mean a thing, Miss Pamela. I just want you to do as I ask."

Burke left Blacon Grange and went back to "The Sickle."

CHAPTER TWENTY-ONE

"ARREST VANCE!"

FOSTER WAS WAITING for Burke in the private room at the inn.

"I've circulated the description, sir, and I have to report that Grainger and his pal, Delisle, have emptied out. Our local man says he saw Delisle's car, Grainger at the wheel, on the main Gloucester road, at seven o'clock last night, licking along at a high speed."

"He didn't see anything of Grenville, then?"

"I asked him that, but there's nothing doing." Grenville's not the type of man to rush headlong into trouble," mused Burke, "and yet, after what that girl told him about Delisle, I wonder. . . ."

"Did you see Birtles, sir?"

"You're wrong there, Forster. You've slipped up. Birtles is not our man . . . a half-brother, so I gathered. Now, how many people could have taken that dagger from Blacon Grange?"

Burke sat down at the table and buried his head in his hands. Then he looked up. "We're leaving this afternoon, Forster. I've got to make a report in person at headquarters."

Four o'clock that same afternoon found Burke closeted with Sir Michael Kenyon.

"I knew you'd do it," exclaimed the A.C. warmly when Burke had finished speaking, "but I'm not so sure that I agree with your magnanimous expression of Vance's innocence. It's the nearest piece of circumstantial evidence I know," he commented. "The old man's in it up to the neck."

"But I don't see that he had any motive, sir," Burke protested. "A man needs a pretty strong motive for murder. And even assuming he had, would he commit a crime with a dagger from his own collection? That's the weakness, sir. There are too many people in Blacon ready to testify to the fact that the weapon was missing."

"I concede your point, Burke, but we must not forget that Vance and Stone were by no means friends, and though Vance appears to have had nothing to gain by the murder, we must not forget that hallucination or an obsession brooded over until it becomes mad-

119

ness frequently plays an important part in crimes that are not obvious. We know so little about the past lives of these men that we cannot judge with any degree of certainty."

"I would suggest, sir, that no action is taken in the matter for the moment."

"You mean arresting Vance? Of course, the position is difficult, and on the face of it, Burke, the man is guilty. Everything points to that. We have to accept his story that he found Stone dead, and even if we agree that he did a logical and human thing in stealing the weapon and concealing it, we have his persistent lies confronting us. In every respect the man has behaved like a criminal. I see no harm in issuing a warrant immediately. If no other purpose were served and your own ideas of the man's innocence prove correct, someone is going to be forced into the open. A man on trial for his life will disclose many secrets."

Burke started. He had expected this, but he had never dreamed that Sir Michael would want to apprehend Vance immediately. Such a course had been right outside the area of his recent calculations.

"If you do that, sir, we shall never find Stone's murderer. Such a course is playing right into the hands of the fiends who planned the whole business. If it comes to Vance's arrest I shall feel called on to hand in my resignation."

Burke's words came quietly yet incisively. There was a note of determination in his voice that caused an uneasiness in the mind of the assistant commissioner.

"Nonsense, Burke," he protested. "What good would resignation do for you? Why, man, you're only at the beginning of your career. One of these days I'd like to stake that you'll be occupying this room as I'm doing now."

"That may or may not be prophetic, sir, but I mean what I say. John Vance is innocent, and if you make the mistake of arresting him our chances of laying the criminal by the heel will be gone. So long as Vance remains at liberty and so long as it would appear that Scotland Yard has drawn off Vance, the sooner will our man show his hand."

"You mean Delisle?"

"I do, sir."

"But on your own admission, Burke, the man has a cast-iron alibi. Even Arsène Lupin was never in two places at once."

"My ultimatum still holds, sir."

"Oh, well, I suppose I'll have to pander to your eccentricity," grumbled Sir Michael, "and I expect that when word of the hash we've made of it comes to the commissioner and the Home Secretary we shall be for the high jump."

"You're forgetting Parliament, sir, *and* the House of Lords," smiled Burke, knowing that he had won his point.

Sir Michael made a peculiar noise that might have been mistaken for derision or even annoyance.

"Get on with it and stop wasting my time," commanded the A.C. "And the next time you come in here don't forget to bring either Vance or . . . or whoever you pick on," he concluded.

Curtis Burke felt inordinately pleased with himself. The interview with Sir Michael had gone as he had hoped it would go.

In his own office Burke immediately sent for Sergeant Forster, who had been told off to round up London inquiries and present a full statement.

Forster came in humming a tune which might have been a hymn or a foxtrot.

"What's the broadcast now?" Burke inquired, swinging around in his chair.

"Very thin programme, sir. Very thin indeed. All holders of Mexican oil stock have been interviewed with the exception of two."

"I gave orders that everyone should be seen," interrupted Burke irritably.

"That was impossible, sir. The people concerned are dead and left no address."

"Cut out the comic stuff, Forster, and let me see the report."

Forster, chastened, handed to Burke a sheaf of papers, all neatly typed.

"Any reply to the newspaper appeal?" he asked.

"None, sir. People don't like to come into the open over things like that. Makes them look mugs. I know I wouldn't."

"Perhaps you're right, Forster. Now, what about our old friend Rodgers?"

Burke glanced through the report of the man who had been guarding Mr. Rodgers as though he were a brother for a week.

Burke had heard a report about the incident down in the tavern by Wapping Steps, but had not been inclined to pay very much attention to it. Men in liquor could not be relied on, and what Rodgers had said to his "friend" was probably nothing more than sheer bravado.

Mr. Rodgers had made a journey each day to the City, presumably in search of further employment. Every day that was, except yesterday, when he had spent the bulk of his time on a round tour of the public-houses, getting himself pleasantly drunk. His "shadow" had reported that this was unusual, for, apart from the incident at Wapping, Rodgers had always appeared the possessor of sober habits.

"We'd better find out where he's getting the money from," instructed Burke. "Withdraw the man you've got on him and take over the job yourself, Forster. Rodgers didn't strike me as the type of man who had saved a great deal of cash. He appeared rather careless."

"It shall be done, sir. I'll take over right away."

"And see if there's anyone at home in Delisle's flat in Jermyn Street. If he's left Blacon he's almost sure to be in town."

Sergeant Forster left Burke to his own devices. He didn't much care for the particular job allotted to him; felt that Burke was being unreasonable in assigning him such a Boy Scout job. It was beneath the dignity of a sergeant of Forster's mentality.

Forster picked up Rodgers' "shadow" an hour later, after a round of telephone calls. The detective was disconsolate. He had left Rodgers' house at nine-thirty that morning. Rodgers had come down to the City as usual and made his round of the stock-jobbers' offices. Then he had boarded a bus for Chelsea in the Strand.

Detective Rafter had boarded the same vehicle. Rodgers had gone upstairs and Rafter had a seat inside close to the door. Half-way along the King's Road the bus pulled up sharply. Rafter looked out to see what was the matter and discovered a second bus drawn up alongside the one in which he was travelling. It appeared that a portion of the roadway was under repair, permitting only one vehicle to pass at a time. The driver of a bus coming from the opposite direction imagined, evidently, that he had the right of way, while a similar thought crossed the mind of the driver of Detective Rafter's bus. As a result of this instance of simultaneous thought a collision was narrowly averted and for a few moments the two buses stood abreast and nearly touching.

Rafter scrutinised the descending passengers at each stop, but there was no sign of Rodgers, and when eventually the vehicle arrived at its destination Rafter was amazed to discover that there were no passengers at all on the top deck. Rodgers had mysteriously vanished.

The truth was that Rodgers was beginning to grow anxious. He had been aware that he was being shadowed. The fact had dawned on him a day or two ago and it was beginning to distress him. There were moments when he found himself being flung into a panic. On several occasion he had endeavoured to throw the watcher off the scent, but he had never been wholly successful. Always the fellow was there, somewhere around the house, waiting for him to begin the trail all over again.

Now Mr. Rodgers particularly wanted to be without an escort this day, and although he knew that Rafter had boarded the bus that he himself had got on, he was determined to outwit the fellow later. His chance came suddenly. It was when the altercation between the two drivers of the buses in the King's Road took place that Rodgers, being perplexed with the problem, decided to take immediate action. He found that the bus proceeding citywards was so close to his own that from the open top he could stretch out a hand and touch its rail. The idea came to him immediately, and before anyone knew what was taking place, Mr. Rodgers had clambered from one bus to the other and, noting that the conductor of his newly acquired chariot was out in the roadway making a personal contribution to the wrangle of the drivers, he sprang lightly down the steps and out into the street.

About half an hour later he approached a large detached house on the far side of Wandsworth Common and entered by the back door. A few minutes later he was talking across a table to Rodney Delisle.

"What the devil did you come here for?" Delisle demanded fiercely. "Are you insane? Didn't you have my instructions? I'll have you know, Rodgers, that when I give instructions, I mean them to be carried out."

"Your instructions were carried out," snarled Rodgers, "and where's it landed me? Trailed around all day and every day by a cop. What sort of a life d'you think mine is? Besides I want some cash. I'm cleaned out."

Delisle's face had grown grey.

"I suppose you've been trailed here, then?"

"D'you think I'm that sort of fool. I've got brains, I have. But you haven't answered my question. What about some cash?"

"You can go to hell, Rodgers," was Delisle's answer.

"When I go to hell, I won't do the trip alone," said Rodgers, with a world of meaning in his tone.

"Threatening, eh? I like your nerve, Rodgers, you little rat. What will you say when I ring up the police?"

"You daren't do that," snapped back Rodgers.

"One never knows what I shall do one of these days," Delisle told him. "You're quite sure no one knows you came here?"

"Not a soul," Rodgers told him, hopefully.

"That's all right for me," flashed Delisle, as he got up and strode from the room. At the door he turned and added: "Because I've a notion that you're going to make that hell trip quicker than you think."

CHAPTER TWENTY-TWO

A PRIVATE PRISON

IAN GRENVILLE FOUND himself a prisoner.

His prison was an attic which, from its appearance, had not been recently converted. The small window in the wall was heavily barred on the inside, although the window itself had never been designed to open. A wooden camp bed occupied one corner of the apartment. In the centre was a rough deal table and a straight-backed chair. The door was a substantial piece of work, with a large and heavy lock, and presumably triple bolts, on the outside. There were no panels in that door—just a solid piece of timber that was likely successfully to resist any efforts he might make to break it down.

The night he had been caught had been an eventful one. Delisle he had found in a particularly nasty mood, and it seemed amazing to Grenville that a man could have such an ugly side to his nature. His language was coarse and his temper vile.

"You came here to spy, did you?" Delisle had said, with a sneer. "Well, you know the penalty for spying, my young fellow. I never permit any spying into my affairs, and those who indulge in the pursuit usually regret the adventure sooner or later. At the moment I haven't quite made up my mind just what to do with you. It all depends on the circumstances," and Delisle had laughed—a harsh, grating kind of laugh that made Ian feel peculiarly chill and shivery.

He had quickly come to the conclusion that the man was a dangerous maniac, and as the bloodshot eyes narrowed in their gaze, he felt that any suspicions he may have had regarding Delisle's complicity in the Stone murder, and his culpability in trying to "frame" Vance, were more than substantiated. That the fellow was abnormal there could be no doubt; that he might not stop even at cold-blooded murder was also a probability. Yet Grenville was far from being afraid. He felt that he had achieved something in following Delisle and Grainger, because Delisle was supposed to have a flat in Jermyn Street, not a mysterious mansion somewhere

125

in the suburbs, where he held nocturnal meetings with as slick a set of crooks as one could wish to find outside the pages of Chicago fiction.

"What do you intend doing with me?" Grenville had asked modestly.

"I tell you I don't know, you fool," Delisle had retorted. "You deserve to be shot—perhaps you will be," he smiled devilishly. "Until I make up my mind you remain here. By the way, have you any money on you? Come on, out with it."

But Ian had not time to comply personally with the request. Two men who had been standing beside the door came forward and conducted a searching inquiry among the contents of his pockets. Delisle snatched up the note-case and tore it open. From it he pulled out four one pound Treasury notes, gazed at them for a moment and then unceremoniously stuffed them into his pocket.

"That'll do," he spat at the two men. "Take him upstairs. There's no need to truss him up. No one ever gets away from here."

So Ian had been taken upstairs and flung into this room. He had felt his way around until he had come upon the bed. There he lay until the dawn broke like a grey phantom stalking silently across the room.

At eight o'clock there had come to his ears the sound of a withdrawal of bolts and a snapping of a key in the lock. A man entered with a plate of bread and a mug of cocoa. Without speaking he placed them on the table in the centre of the room and with a glance at the man on the bed immediately withdrew, locking and bolting the door behind him again.

The situation in Grenville's mind was fantastic. It savoured more of a page from fiction than from real life, and as yet he was unaware of what his particular crime might be. His brain was swimming with theories; some of them were spectacular ones in which he saw Delisle as the head of a great international gang of thieves, murderers and blackmailers. He was aware that such gangs existed. He had read about them in the newspapers, but for the life of him he could not connect Delisle's London activities with the affair at Blacon and the murder of Martin Stone that Burke was investigating. Yet there obviously must be some connection, else Delisle would not take such pains to limit his freedom in the way he was doing.

And to think that this scoundrel was engaged to Pamela Vance. The thought made him shiver. Of course, it was absurd. The whole thing was more like a dream than stern reality. Once or twice he had actually stretched out his arm to make quite sure it was not a nightmare from which he was suffering.

Towards midday the door opened again and Delisle entered.

He was debonair as usual, in faultlessly-cut clothes and well-groomed. Ian Grenville, in his crumpled suit and unshaven face, felt annoyingly inferior and at a tremendous disadvantage.

"There are one or two things I forgot to ask you last night," Delisle began calmly, but with a steely edge to his words. "The first is, how much do you know about Vance and his daughter—how much have they told you?"

"Nothing at all," lied Grenville coldly. "Miss Vance had so little time for talking to me."

"You can cut out all that," Delisle remarked savagely. "You do know something, and I'm going to find out how much it is. If, as you say, you know nothing, what was your object in sneaking into my car last night and following me here?"

"Just curiosity," smiled Grenville.

"And may I ask if that curiosity is satisfied?"

"Partly, Mr. Delisle. I have the advantage of seeing you as you really are and not as people in Blacon imagine you to be."

Grenville regretted the taunt almost before the words had left his lips. It was little use trying to fence with Delisle, and it led him nowhere.

"So you think you know, eh?" snarled Delisle, advancing to where Grenville was sitting on the edge of the low bed. "Well, take that and see something else," and before Grenville could offer any defence the man's fist shot out and caught him full between the eyes. With a groan the younger man fell backwards and lay still. For a moment Delisle stood over the prostrate form of Grenville with a cynical and malicious smile on his face.

"And there's much more than that coming to you, my cock sparrow; or to anyone else who cares to butt into my affairs uninvited," and with that he went from the room.

~ ~ ~ ~ ~

Sergeant Forster was particularly scathing when he heard Constable Rafter's story of the disappearance of Mr. Rodgers. What Sergeant Forster had to say about the efficiency of the C.I.D. constables would be an education to any professor of essentially modern languages.

"And now I suppose I've got to find him myself," grumbled the sergeant, "and all because . . . but what's the use? We all have our trials and tribulations."

It was little wonder that Sergeant Forster, when he returned to Scotland Yard at nine o'clock that night, was in an ill humour. He had drawn a definite blank at Jermyn Street. True, he had found the flat rented by Delisle, but the caretaker had told him that Mr. Delisle had not been to the place more than three times the whole summer. The last time, it appeared, was two months ago, when he spent the night there and went away early the following morning. What was Mr. Delisle like? Did he have many visitors to the flat? The caretaker could not say for sure. Delisle had always been easy to get along with, and if he ever had visitors they were certainly not the kind that caused any apprehension in the mind of the caretaker.

Forster went away, grumbling to himself. He couldn't understand Inspector Burke's methods of working at all. Why, here was a clear-cut case against John Vance—as clear as any policeman could wish for. Why should he, Sergeant Forster, be condemned to chase his tail around London? Now, had it been Grainger or Birtles, Sergeant Forster could have understood it better. Particularly had it been Grainger! One of these days he must hunt up Grainger. The fellow might be worth a visit, if only to renew old acquaintance. It would be quite like old times. As for Rodgers . . . once again Sergeant Forster's vocabulary came to his aid in his hour of trial. He had argued with Burke until he was blue in the neck about Rodgers. The fellow was of no consequence at all . . . simply didn't count.

Burke was still at his desk when Forster entered and told his tale of woe.

"That's too bad," consoled Burke, "but I did think Rafter had more in him than to lose his man like that. But what's the worry? Rodgers will be back home again tonight and we'll bring him down here in the morning for a little private chat."

But things did not work out quite that way at all. Mr. Rodgers did not return home that night. Neither was he seen at any of his favourite hostelries. But at eleven-thirty that night a body was taken from the river in the neighbourhood of Battersea Bridge.

Burke received the call at the Yard, and Forster was still with him bemoaning his bad luck.

"Come on," called Burke, "we're going to Battersea."

"What for?" asked Forster. "I feel more like going to bed."

"They've taken a body from the river," explained Burke, "and the inspector says he has a notion it's Rodgers."

But even that information did not ignite a spark of enthusiasm in the sergeant's breast. He whistled sadly as he followed the inspector from the building.

CHAPTER TWENTY-THREE

WHO KILLED RODGERS?

THE DIVISIONAL POLICE surgeon was busy in the police hut when Burke and Forster arrived. Burke glanced down at the form on the floor. It was Rodgers sure enough.

"Well, Doctor, what's the result?" asked Burke.

The D.P.S. looked up. "Shot through the heart," he said laconically. "He was certainly dead before he went in the water."

"How long ago?"

"Probably five or six hours; may have been longer."

"Got the bullet?"

The medical man shook his head. "It passed right through," he told them.

"Would it be from a Browning, do you think?"

"Very likely. Might have been of any type, of course.

Burke turned to Forster grimly.

"Our assassin has come to Town," he remarked.

Forster nodded absently. He was very tired, and now that Rodgers had passed from requiring further trailing he felt more at his ease.

"Circulate all stations," commanded Burke to the inspector in charge. "I want to know where this man was last seen and by whom."

"Still got notions about Rodgers, Chief?" asked Forster as they went on to the waiting motor-car.

"And why not?" demanded Burke impatiently. "Someone evidently thought him important, even if you didn't."

For answer the sergeant shrugged his square shoulders and sighed.

Back at Scotland Yard, Burke set to work again. He was awaiting a reply from his cable to San Luis, regarding a secret society formed there somewhere about thirty years ago.

"You'd better go and get some sleep," he advised Forster, and for the first time that night a smile appeared on the face of the disgruntled sergeant.

"That's what I would call the best speech of the evening," he smiled. "I'll report for duty any time after six o'clock tomorrow morning."

Burke heard the door close softly. "Poor old Forster—one of the old school—couldn't see more than a yard or so beyond his nose. Well, times had changed and so had methods. Burke had now almost completed an extravagant theory. He had decided that his man was Rodney Delisle, but how to get him was another matter. His alibi on the night of the crime was watertight. It would be upheld in any court of law. But there must be a loophole somewhere. If neither Delisle nor Vance had killed Stone, who had?

Stone had been struck down from behind. If anyone had entered Stone's office, Stone, if he were seated at his desk, must have seen him. Had the person entering been a stranger to Stone, it was unlikely that he could have got around the desk to strike the blow without being observed. The room contained only one door. Therefore, Burke argued, it must have been someone familiar to the dead man. He must also be someone in the habit of entering that room and used to moving around it freely. Could it have been Rodgers, the clerk?

The thought stimulated him. Rodgers was Stone's chief clerk. Perhaps on the night of the crime Rodgers had occasion to work rather later than usual. Stone would remain in the office because he was expecting Vance to call on him at about six-thirty or seven o'clock. No, that wasn't quite right. Stone had been out of town that afternoon. Rodgers had said so. He returned about six-fifteen, presumably for the interview with Vance. It was possible that Rodgers had waited for him after the other members of the staff had gone.

That sounded all right in theory, but there was the weapon to be considered. How did Rodgers (if his theory that the chief clerk was the culprit was correct) get hold of the dagger which had been established as belonging to the Vance collection?

Further than that, the print men had reported that the only finger marks found on the haft of the dagger had been those belonging to Vance himself. Burke had frowned at that report. It was tragically disturbing. He must not show it to Sir Michael Kenyon just yet. Vance had sworn to him that he had never touched that dagger with his naked fingers. What could it mean? If Vance was telling the truth, those finger-prints must be old ones, and the person who I had taken that weapon from Blacon Grange had exercised the utmost caution in filching it from its place in the rack.

Burke puzzled over the problem well into the night. It was possible, of course, that Delisle had taken the weapon. Delisle had ample opportunity for that. He was a constant visitor to Blacon Grange. Yet there was no suggestion of a liaison between Delisle and Rodgers. That was the puzzling part of the problem. During his inquisitions Rodgers had not even mentioned that he was in any way acquainted with Delisle, but Burke remembered that Rodgers had never been specifically questioned on that point, and now that Rodgers had passed out there was no likelihood of finding out whether the pair were known to one another or not.

In the midst of this pondering a reply came from San Luis. The police had no record of any such society as he had mentioned in his communication to them.

Burke flung the reply on his desk with a gesture of annoyance. He had half suspected that when the reply came it would not be helpful.

An hour later Burke was in his bed and, like Sergeant Forster, he was fast asleep.

The telephone bell tinkled on the table beside his bed. Lifting off the receiver, he heard the voice of Sergeant Pace, who had assisted him earlier in the inquiry.

"There's a woman down here, sir, asking to see you. She says her name is Marcelle Merlin and she says she must speak to you."

Burke replaced the receiver with a frown. Marcelle . . . where had he heard the name before? Ah! She was the writer of one of the letters he had found in Stone's desk . . . an importunate lady, if he remembered rightly.

In half an hour he was seated at his desk, talking to a well-dressed woman of about thirty-five with dark, flashing eyes and a nice taste in perfume.

"It's about Rodgers," she said, speaking rapidly and agitatedly. "In the newspapers this morning . . . his death I mean. . . . He promised to call on me last night."

Burke eyed the woman carefully.

"I'm afraid I can't see what I can do," he told her guardedly. "I'm just as sorry as you are that Mr. Rodgers met his death in the unhappy manner he has. But perhaps you have come to tell me who it was killed him?"

"That I can't do, Mr. Burke. All I know is that Rodgers was working for someone. He hinted as much. My only interest in him is that he owed me money."

"How long have you known Rodgers?"

"About two years. But why ask that?"

"You knew Martin Stone, didn't you?" he asked, thinking that her friendships had come to singularly unfortunate endings.

She nodded.

"He was a bad egg, Mr. Burke. He let me down, and I wasn't the only woman."

"Really, this is most interesting, Mrs. Merlin, because you once wrote a particularly disagreeable letter to Stone, didn't you?"

In a flash the woman realised her mistake and tried to cover it up.

"Oh, that," she smiled. "Stone was a natural coward where women were concerned. He promised me three hundred pounds and never paid up. Wasn't it proper that I should write and demand it?"

"I suppose you were within your rights," returned Burke, with apparent carelessness. "Rather an unsavoury business, I gather?"

"No more than usual," she told him with a curl of her upper lip.

"May I ask what your object was in coming to see me?" asked Burke.

"I want to know who killed Rodgers," she said bluntly.

"Another question, Mrs. Merlin. How did Rodgers get into your debt?"

"I hope you won't think ill of me, Mr. Burke," she said after a pause. "I first met Rodgers in a restaurant in the Strand. I was naturally interested when he told me that he worked for Stone, and I gathered, too, that he hated his employer. He told me that Stone had cheated him out of a large sum of money on some stock exchange dealings. He was very sore was Mr. Rodgers. Then I thought of a way to hit back at Stone and at the same time earn an honest copper or two. I promised Rodgers to provide him with some first-class scandal evidence about Stone on condition that he paid me for it.

"Rodgers jumped at the offer. I wasn't in the least interested to know how he obtained the money so long as I got it."

"How much did you want?" asked Burke.

"Fifty pounds, and it was cheap at the price."

"And did he pay you?"

"He did, Mr. Burke—paid in notes."

"What was the date of this interesting transaction?"

"The Sunday night before Stone was killed," she told him in a low voice.

"And you think. . . ."

"I can't think," she broke out fiercely. "Rodgers was a nice little fellow. I liked him. We were going to be married."

"I still fail to understand the object of this visit," Burke persisted.

"I want to know who killed him!" she demanded passionately. "I want to get even—see!"

"And you imagine I know the answer to your question?"

"Aren't you as likely to know as anyone?"

"Not so likely as the one who committed the crime," retorted Burke. "Now listen to me, Mrs. Merlin. Did you ever hear Rodgers speak of a man named Delisle?"

"Delisle!" The woman's lips formed the name hoarsely. "You don't mean that he—that he is in this business. I never thought of that. But it's possible, Mr. Burke. I think I begin to see it now. Rodgers would never tell me some of the things I wanted to know."

"You know Delisle?" Burke tried to keep a level note in his voice.

"I've never met him, if that's what you mean. But I've heard of him. Surely Scotland Yard know all there is to know about that man?"

Burke shook his head. "Not yet, Mrs. Merlin, but with your help we soon shall."

"No, no, no!" she cried desperately. "I can't tell you—I dare not." Burke was quickly conscious of fear in the woman's voice.

"Who and what is Delisle?" Burke demanded imperiously.

The woman covered her face with her hands and sobbed hysterically.

Then she looked up at him.

"No one really knows for sure," she told him unsteadily, "except that he's a big man in his way. Head of a syndicate . . . but surely. . . ."

"Thank you, Mrs. Merlin. I begin to see daylight, and I assure you that once I have laid hands on the person who killed Rodgers I shall, I hope, have also found the person who was responsible for the murder of Stone."

She dropped her eyes before the inspector's penetrating gaze.

"I don't think so," she whispered hoarsely. "He's dead, Mr. Burke . . . beyond the Law."

There was a tense silence in the room for a moment; then Burke said: "Did Rodgers confess to you, then?"

Panic filled the woman's eyes.

"No," she cried, "he never said a word—it is only a woman's intuition."

"Thank you, Mrs. Merlin. I will give you my promise that you won't be dragged into all this. By the way, have I ever met Mr. Merlin?"

For the first time during the interview the woman smiled. She flung back her head.

"I should say not," she flashed. "He hasn't been born yet."

CHAPTER TWENTY-FOUR

DELISLE SHOWS HIS HAND

JOHN VANCE SAT in his study, reading. Pamela had gone over to Hereford for the express purpose of shopping. She told him she hoped to return home in good time for dinner. An hour before someone had telephoned Pamela, but had been told that she was not at home. Birtles had taken the call and appeared surprised when the caller did not give any name nor leave any message.

As for Vance, while his mind was more at peace than it had been for more than a week, he was still haunted by the fear that in some way he might become caught in the net of the law.

No one realised more than he did himself how the fates had plotted against him; and no one knew the sleepless nights and the hours of mental anguish he had endured. They say that innocence implies an untroubled conscience, but John Vance knew differently. He was innocent of the murder of Martin Stone, and yet on the evidence the law had everything it required to arraign him on a charge of murder, and he—he only had his own unsupported word to lay against the charge.

Since he had been persuaded to unburden himself to Inspector Curtis Burke he had felt considerably easier in his mind, but even that confession had not erased from his awareness the still terrible position in which he was placed. Burke had said he believed him innocent, but Vance knew that Burke had to prove that innocence before the powers-that-be at Scotland Yard would be prepared to obliterate his name from their pages of evidence.

Pamela, too, was feeling the strain. If it hadn't been for his daughter John Vance did not know where he would have been or what he might have done. Pamela had been a tower of strength because she believed in him. And now there was this other anxiety—the disappearance of Ian Grenville. Vance had always liked the boy—liked him better than he had ever liked Rodney Delisle. But his own likes and dislikes counted for nothing. It was for Pamela to make her own choice, and oddly enough she had chosen Delisle.

When she had told him of her engagement Vance had expressed neither surprise nor comment. If Delisle was Pamela's choice he was content. Yet he had pondered over it. He remembered that Pamela had referred to it quite casually, just as if it were something of no importance. And he had not seen Delisle since; which he considered was rather odd. He often told himself that there was something of a mystery about the affair, but he had not yet brought himself to the point of tackling the girl on the subject.

Pamela was all he had, and he wanted her to be happy. Sometimes he wondered whether she would be really happy with Delisle; or would it have been better if Grenville. . . . Vance found his thoughts running away with him this afternoon. Funny, he thought, only a week ago since he had set out for London to meet Stone. It seemed more like a year. In seven days he had known the deepest depths of remorse; had been lowered into the dry wells of anxiety and fear; seen a challenging look—fleeting though it had been—in the eyes of his daughter when he had told her he had not spoken the truth about last Tuesday. And now Grenville. . . .

Pamela had appeared oddly upset when Burke had brought the news to them; which was all the more curious, since she was engaged to be married to Delisle. Vance was forced to admit that he did not understand the modern young woman. Dash it all, if she liked Grenville better than she liked Delisle, why had she promised herself to him? It was a riddle he quite frankly did not understand, and the more he gave his thoughts to it the less intelligible it became.

He had not heard from Burke since the inspector's departure for London yesterday morning. Delisle had gone away, too, so he had heard. But nevertheless he had not forgotten Burke's injunction. No one must know that Burke knew his secret.

Vance was wondering whether Burke would or would not be successful in clearing up the mystery at the London end when Birtles announced that Mr. Delisle had called.

Delisle came in with a smile on his lips and sank down into a chair opposite to Vance with the glowing fire between them, for the day was grey and there was a chill in the wind.

"I hear Pamela's out," he mentioned casually as he took a cigarette from Vance's proffered case, "but perhaps that's just as well. As a matter of fact, Vance, old man, I want to have a little private chat with you."

"Carry on, my boy," smiled Vance indulgently, yet wondering what it all meant.

"I assure you that I find it rather difficult to make a beginning," Delisle said guardedly. "As a matter of fact I was wondering if you could help me. After all, sir, your daughter is going to marry me some day."

Vance regarded his visitor with quiet, unconcerned interest.

"How much do you want?" asked Vance quietly.

The interview was proving easier than Delisle had expected.

"About a couple of thousand," he smiled. "I've had a few 'flops' in the past month or so, and I'm rather tight."

"Nothing doing," intimated Vance with the same cool uncon-cern. "I've ceased being a moneylender, Even if you were my son-in-law—which you are not as yet—I should think very care-fully before I broke a rule of a lifetime—more or less."

John Vance was watching Delisle covertly. He noticed a subtle change come over the man's features and he sensed that trouble was brewing.

"So that's how things are, eh, Vance?" responded Delisle on a much less friendly note. "You don't care to trust me. Is that it?"

"It's not a question of trust at all," Vance endeavoured to ex-plain. "Rather is it a matter of principle."

"You really mean that?"

"Absolutely!"

"That's where you're wrong, Vance. You're going to pay me that two thousand pounds before I leave this house."

"You surprise me, Delisle. And by what method am I to be thus relieved?"

"There is only one method, Vance. Now listen to me. You may know that the detective Burke from Scotland Yard has gone back to London. But do you know why he has gone back? You don't! Well, I'll tell you. He's gone back because he is defeated. You've won the first round, Vance. To all intents and purposes Scotland Yard has given the case up. You won't be worried any more by those devilish awkward questions Burke always asks."

"Really!" exclaimed Vance, amused. "This is first-rate news. I suppose you have this on sound authority?"

"Straight from the mouth of the animal itself," Delisle informed him. "You've been struck off the list. But—and I want you to pay particular attention to what I am going to say—though you have succeeded in bluffing Burke and Scotland Yard with your story of gazing at the stars all last Tuesday night, you can't bluff me. You went to London last Tuesday night, Vance, and while you were in London you killed Martin Stone. How's that?"

"That's quite a good one. I must try to remember it and tell it to my friends," smiled Vance easily.

"Stop fooling and let's get to business," growled Delisle, unable to understand the geniality of the man opposite him. "And what would the police say if they knew you had received a letter instructing you to kill Stone under a deed of obligation which you entered into thirty years ago out in San Luis? What would they say to that? I'll tell you what they'd say. They'd say: 'Bring in Vance. He's the man we've been looking for all the time.' "

Delisle paused for a moment, anxious to observe the effect of his words. But Vance was only smiling—still smiling that enigmatical and aggravating smile.

"And they'd take you in, Vance. They'd set you up in court before a judge and a jury. They'd tell the judge and jury that you had a good reason for wishing Stone dead, and that you had answered the call from Mexico. They'd tell the judge and jury that out in Mexico Stone had once had to run the gauntlet. His name stank in the nostrils of every decent-minded Mexican. He was the originator of the white slave traffic for the American seaport towns, and you knew. You knew that, Vance, and you waited—you waited to strike and you struck. Now do you realise why you must pay me two thousand pounds right now?"

"What a harrowing story, Delisle. You might yet make a novelist with an imagination like that. But I'm interrupting you. Please proceed!"

"Damn it, man! Can't you understand? Or is it that you don't want to understand?"

"I only appreciate that you are asking for two thousand pounds that I have not the least intention of giving you."

"Then by tomorrow morning I shall place the full facts in the hands of the police."

Vance started and Delisle was quick to notice it.

"That rattles you, eh? Well, there's yet time. How about handing it over?"

For answer Vance smiled and shook his head.

"The bluff won't work, Delisle. I'm not afraid of the police any longer, but I'll tell you this, and now it's my turn to do a spot of talking. I should say that if you were to go too close to Scotland Yard you might find the neighbourhood distinctly unhealthy. Now get out, d'you hear? GET OUT, or I'll fling you out with my own hands."

Vance sprang to his feet and stood over Delisle menacingly.

The man's face went livid with rage. He had been cheated—cheated, and it had all seemed so absurdly easy. This man had been toying with him; performing the old cat and mouse trick.

"It would give me great pleasure to shoot you," snarled Delisle as he slunk away towards the door.

"I shouldn't try that if I were you; the police may still be close at hand. You'd forgotten that, eh? What if I told you they were listening in to our friendly little chat. . . ."

But Delisle was not listening. He was out in the hall, snatching his coat and hat and a moment later he was running down the drive like a scared animal.

When he had gone Vance's face grew serious. He remembered Inspector Burke's words: "The criminal will come out into the open. He will show his hand."

Making up his mind swiftly, Vance crossed the hall to the telephone and asked for Whitehall 1212.

CHAPTER TWENTY-FIVE

NEW CLUES

CURTIS BURKE HAPPENED to be at Scotland Yard when John Vance's message was put through. He listened intently while Vance told him everything that had occurred during Delisle's visit.

"I think I can safely leave you to deal with him, Mr. Vance," called Burke. "In any event, I doubt whether you will be troubled with him again, but you see what you have saved yourself simply because you had the courage in the end to tell me everything."

Vance replied that he certainly did see, and hoped that Burke would have little difficulty in laying hands on the scoundrel before it was too late.

But Burke was not in the least optimistic of securing Delisle. Attempted blackmail was serious, but no jury would convict on uncorroborated evidence such as only Vance would supply. At first Burke thought of advising Vance to agree to pay the money, after first mentioning that he had been thinking things over and had come to the conclusion that Delisle was right. But on second thoughts he knew that Delisle would not expose himself to any danger, and the money would be lost without anything gained; perhaps, indeed, it might aid the said Mr. Delisle to escape justice altogether!

The difficulty which now confronted Burke was that Delisle appeared to be nowhere in London. Burke had secretly circulated the man's description, not for arrest, but for watching and report, and he still had hopes that some news of him would arrive. The Blacon police force knew nothing. Burke hardly anticipated that they would. How were Sergeant Mulliver and his assistant to know just the precise moment that Delisle would turn up and in what manner?

But there was something more important than that. Burke did not want Delisle brought in on a charge of blackmail. When he did get him, he wanted him on a charge of murder, and possibly as an accessory to another.

Burke had been sorting through the contents of Rodgers' pockets when Vance had called him up on the telephone.

The miscellaneous collection was spread out on his desk in front of him, but Burke had so far failed to discover anything of value in connection with the case.

Then he alighted on something that might or might not possess some particular significance. It was a small screw of paper which had been found deep in the corner of one of the pocket linings. Carefully Burke unrolled it. Unfortunately it was not in one piece. Evidently Rodgers, having jotted something down, or perhaps having been given it to memorise, had torn it into fragments and screwed the whole or part of it together in this fashion.

Burke laid the small fragments of paper out on the desk and noted that there was some pencilling on them. Unfortunately one piece was missing—the vital piece, so it happened; a piece that should have been across the centre, thus leaving a gap which had to be filled in somehow if the address—he was sure it was an address—was to be deciphered. As he looked at it, it appeared as follows:

8, Bes   *h Rd.*
    Take No.   *s.*

That was all, and it was going to be a problem for the inquiries sergeant and his staff to provide a few alternatives, particularly as there was no indication as to whether the address was in London or elsewhere.

Still, it was something, because Burke had an idea that it was at this address that the unfortunate Rodgers had met his death.

Sergeant Forster came in to say that so far no report had been received concerning the missing Delisle.

"I've been round to see whether my friend 'Scully' Grainger is at any of his usual haunts. He's not there. No one's seen 'Scully' for months. I was told at one pub that 'Scully' was now a reformed character and was living in Reformation Row."

"Where's that?" asked the inspector innocently.

"We've got a job on tonight, Forster," he continued with a grin. "A little job of burglary—breaking in. Give Dutton a ring. He's the best lock-picker on the staff, isn't he?"

"He is, sir," admitted Forster. "I'd back old Dutton to pick all the locks in Dartmoor in half an hour."

Twenty minutes later three police officers set off by police car to Jermyn Street. They alighted at the corner and completed the journey on foot.

Flat Number 37 presented no difficulties to the skilled manipulations of Mr. Dutton, who had been picking locks ever since he could remember picking anything, as they said of him.

"No more noise than necessary," cautioned Burke. "You, Dutton, remain out in the vestibule, and if you hear anyone coming turn off the main switch. We'll understand and take cover. Do the same yourself. If Delisle should chance along he might not like to meet us. Forster, you come with me. We want this job over as soon as possible. If we don't find anything here, my name's 'Mud' in the morning or afternoon or whenever the A.C. takes it into his head to send for me."

This was a job after Forster's own heart. He delighted in prying into other people's belongings, and had a secret belief that the furniture in crooks' houses was never so innocent as it seemed.

The apartment was admirably and tastefully furnished.

Burke, eyeing the decorations, turned to Forster and said: "Don't do any more damage to the upholstery than you can help or the hire firm might make an objection."

Forster, eyeing a sumptuous ottoman, grunted his disapproval. Burke turned his attention to a small writing-table in the window. It was unlocked, and he rummaged in the drawers quite happily. The papers he found there were mostly unpaid accounts. In fact he never remembered having seen such a miscellaneous and representative collection before in any one place or belonging to any one person. Rodney Delisle apparently never believed in paying so long as anyone was fool enough to give him credit.

Turning, he saw that Forster was having a roaring time with the ottoman. He was feeling down among the springs as if he were judging at a feather pillow contest.

"Having a good time, Forster?" he inquired sociably.

"A wonderful time, Chief. There's room enough here to hide the crown jewels. I must remember this when I take on the job."

Burke was disappointed as a result of his investigation of the writing-table. The blotting paper, too, was innocent of blemish. Nothing was hidden between its layers. Then he heard Forster give a whoop of delight.

"What's gone wrong?" asked Burke smiling. "Something sting you?"

"There's something here, sir," he intimated eagerly. Forster was still among the springs, but so far he had not defaced the upholstery.

Burke crossed to where he was working and allowed Forster to place his hand deep down between the back and the spring cushions. Burke certainly felt something there, but not possessing the same artistic touch as his colleague, he did not pass an opinion. Forster took from his pocket a large hack knife and honed it on his large hand.

"Here goes," he announced, but no sooner had he uttered the words than the lights were extinguished.

Burke heard a smothered and rather inelegant curse from Forster.

"Get somewhere," whispered Burke, which was easier said than done for a man of Forster's proportions. Burke himself had noted the existence of a lacquered Japanese screen at the far end of the room and crept towards it, feeling his way carefully in the darkness.

The minutes seemed interminable, and then there came a knocking on the door. Receiving no reply, a key was inserted in the lock. The door opened, and then Burke heard the sounds of a scuffle. Pulling his torch from his pocket, he made his way to the hall, where two figures were rolling over and over on the floor. One of them was certainly Dutton, but the other was a little elderly man whom Burke had never seen before.

Pushing on the main switch and turning on the vestibule light, Burke surveyed the mêlée.

Just then Forster came out. "It's all right, Dutton," he announced, taking a look at the intruder. "You've only got the caretaker, and, as his name implies, you mustn't be rough with him."

Explanations followed. The caretaker had been returning home and noticed a light through a crack in the blind, and as the tenant was considerably in arrear with the rent, he had deemed it advisable to make a discreet inquiry.

With a grunt Forster returned to his ottoman.

Ten minutes later Burke was scrutinising an interesting document. It was a list of names of members of the Society for the Purification of Mexico, and among those names was that of John Vance.

~ ~ ~ ~ ~

Ian Grenville was at his wits' ends. He had seen no one except his gaoler for forty-eight hours, and he was beginning to grow apprehensive. The indecision was beginning to pall. His nerves were frayed. If only Delisle would decide what was going to happen to him! No one seemed to be caring. What was Burke doing . . . that redoubtable stalwart from Scotland Yard? Could a fellow disappear like this without hope of being found? It seemed incredible, and yet that was what had happened to him! What would Pamela be thinking? His heart froze at the thought of her at the mercy of Delisle. He cursed himself for a fool in not having told Burke everything on Sunday afternoon.

The man who brought him his meagre rations was wholly uncommunicative. Not a word could be drawn out of him; not a single syllable in response to Grenville's bitter invective.

Then the incredible happened. He had a visit from Delisle himself. Delisle was smiling good-humouredly.

"I don't think I shall have to detain you much longer, Grenville," he began. "I'm making arrangements to go abroad for a short period on business, and that being so, I shall be closing up the house and dismissing the staff."

Hope began to dawn in Grenville's heart, and he noticed that Delisle had a pad of writing paper in one hand and a pen and ink in the other. For a moment he was tempted to attack the fellow, but remembrance of the other occasion restrained him.

"I thought perhaps you would like to write to your father," he smiled. "Here is paper, pen and ink. I want you to tell him that you are safe; that there is no occasion for alarm; that your health is good and that you are happy. You will not, of course, indicate where you are. Not that you could do that, could you? However, I will wait while you write and see that the letter is duly posted."

Grenville, hardly believing his ears, walked to the table and wrote a note to his father, taking care to say precisely the things Delisle had indicated. After all, it was better that his father should receive some sort of letter from him, and to attempt to write what he really wanted would have been so much waste of time with Delisle standing there, almost literally over him. When he had finished he handed the letter to the man across the table.

"You're not cheating me, Delisle?" he asked sharply.

"My dear boy, why should I do that? Is that all the thanks I get? I must really write to the papers about the manners of our Cambridge men."

He took the letter and without further word went out of the room.

In a room on the floor below Granger was waiting for him.

"Here you are," he said surlily, tossing the envelope on the table. "Get busy."

Grainger took the missive and laid it under a sheet of plain glass on the table. Then he took a magnifying glass and looked at the handwriting closely.

Having done that, the man whom Sergeant Forster knew as "Scully" Grainger did as Delisle had commanded him.

He "got busy"!

CHAPTER TWENTY-SIX

PAMELA GOES TO THE RESCUE

PAMELA WAS AWAKE early the following morning. She had heard from Birtles that Delisle had paid a visit to Blacon Grange the previous afternoon and had asked her father about it. He had given her a brief account of what had occurred and he had regarded her shrewdly during the recital.

It was then that she had told him the truth about her reported engagement. Vance looked startled at her account, but in the light of what had happened since he was by no means quite so startled as he might otherwise have been.

"I've finished with him, Daddy," Pamela had said. "Right from the beginning I'd finished with him. But you see how I had to humour him. That afternoon at his cottage I saw him probably as you saw him. I do wish we could get news of Ian."

"I have great faith in Inspector Burke," her father had said. "He's the type of man who never appears to be getting anywhere and yet he gets there every time."

Before going to bed Pamela had rung up Scotland Yard and asked to speak to Inspector Burke, but she was told that the inspector was not in. No. They hadn't heard anything about Mr. Grenville, but it was understood that Inspector Burke had hopes that some news would come through at any moment.

Pamela had not slept any too well that night and felt that she would like a sharp, swift canter before breakfast. On her way along the road she encountered the postman on his cycle. He touched his cap as she reined in and inquired whether there was anything in the mail for her. The postman hunted in his canvas bag, untied a piece of string from a bundle and drew out a letter.

"Here you are, Miss Pamela. Only one this morning!"

He handed it over to her. "I'll be taking the others up to the Grange," he said.

Still seated on her horse, Pamela looked hard at the handwriting on the envelope. It appeared curiously familiar, and as most women

146

do in a similar situation, she insisted on cudgelling her brains to decide who was her correspondent instead of slitting open the envelope and taking the short cut to conviction.

Yes! It was Ian's handwriting. She was sure of that. Last year when she had gone over to Germany he had written her some stunning letters from home. She had enjoyed them immensely.

Tearing open the envelope, she pulled from its caress a single sheet of notepaper—ordinary plain white notepaper—and read:

My dear Pamela,—I am taking a great risk in writing this, but I have managed to make friends with the man who is looking after me. I've promised that should I get free I'll help him . . . give him a job on the estate or something because he's sick of being dependent "on the gang" who employ him. He's going to smuggle this out, because tomorrow night we'll have the house to ourselves and he says it will be a good chance to get out. He's fixing all that, but someone will have to be waiting with a car at the corner of Eltham Road, Wandsworth, on the right-hand side from the main road. This is where you can help me. Can you possibly get along in the car and be there at eleven-thirty prompt, as everything here has to be done to schedule. One important thing must not be overlooked. You mustn't say a word to anyone, not even to your father. My guard says that if a whisper were to leak out they would undoubtedly shoot me. If you value my life, please keep your lips sealed. You won't fail me, I know.

Yours always,
Ian.

Pamela felt herself trembling violently with excitement as she read the instructions over and over again. There was no doubt at all in her mind. This was Ian's writing—there couldn't possibly be any trick about it. The girl felt thrilled. Never before had she realised how much she loved Ian Grenville. He was in danger. She knew that from the style of his letter as much as from its contents. It was not Ian's usual flowing, easy style. He must be dreadfully agitated —dreadfully upset. He depended on her to help him to escape. Once again she consulted the letter and felt that she could almost recite it from memory. He hadn't given her any indication as to the identity of "they," but what did that matter? Perhaps he didn't really know. Perhaps his friend-in-need would not allow him to give the "gang" away. It was going to be a great adventure, the rescuing of

Ian—dear Ian! She had never really appreciated until now what a darling he was!—and when she had carried it through successfully she would be able to teach Inspector Burke something about his own job.

The day died slowly, as days will when one is waiting for the time to pass. She had worked it all out. After lunch she would take out the car, telling her father that she was going over to the Forest of Dean, where she had some friends, and would probably be back later that same evening after dinner. He would not think it particularly strange. He knew she was restless and troubled and would think it best for her to be in young company.

Giving herself plenty of time, she judged that she would be in London in plenty of time for the rendezvous.

She reached London in good time, had a meal in the City, and at ten o'clock set out for the location in Wandsworth. It was a district which she did not know intimately, but a friendly policeman on the Clapham Road was kind enough to direct her to Eltham Road. She arrived there just as a clock at hand was chiming eleven o'clock. Keeping to the directions which Ian had given, she drove the car along until she came to the right-hand corner. She drew up beside the kerb and waited with her engine switched off.

The clock on the dash ticked away the minutes, and she watched the hands anxiously. Everyone who passed unknowingly gave her a joyous thrill, and every moment she anticipated seeing Ian dashing blindly around the corner, wrenching open the door, slamming it behind him and bidding her "drive like the devil."

But nothing quite like that happened.

Instead, someone came quietly to the side of the car where she was sitting with the window lowered and said: "Excuse me, but are you Miss Vance—Miss Pamela Vance?"

Pamela admitted she was.

"Mr. Grenville says will you please come with me to the corner —the second corner, Miss. May I get inside beside you?"

"Certainly." The girl was quivering with semi-suppressed excitement.

The man came around the back of the car and opened the door of the driving compartment. He closed it quietly behind him and sat down.

Pamela had switched on the engine, pressed the starter, heard the rhythm of the engine waiting to be revved into vibrant life, when suddenly there was a movement beside her and the next moment something wet and sticky was pressed against her face. Instinctively she threw up her gloved hands to ward off the attack, but though she struggled she quickly realised—in an increasingly blurred kind of fantasy—that any effort she made was abortive. Slowly she sank into that queer scented oblivion.

The man who had been responsible for this outrage calmly allowed the limp body of the girl to fall naturally down out of view from the side window; wound up that window; slowly yet laboriously transposed the position—his position with that of the girl—until she was slumped down in the seat he had originally occupied, and then putting the car into first gear, let in the clutch, sounded the electric horn and the car glided smoothly away.

When Pamela regained her senses she found herself lying on a low divan in an oddly furnished room. She was alone and it was broad daylight. She felt sick and dizzy and her head swayed, and slowly she tried to collect her scattered thoughts. Gradually mental continuity was achieved. The letter . . . the drive to London . . . the wait at the corner . . . the man who had got into the car beside her . . . his request that she should drive on around the corner because it would be easier for Ian . . . the pressure of the sickly wet pad against her face . . . her wild fight to ward off the danger and then . . . this.

A few minutes after she regained consciousness someone entered the room. It was a blousy-looking woman bearing a cup of tea.

"Here you are, my dear. Just drink this. It'll do you no end of good."

The woman drew a chair beside the divan and stirred the tea for her.

"Where am I, and what is the meaning of this?" demanded Pamela, struggling to raise herself into a sitting position.

"Don't ask me, my dear. I've lived here for six months, and if I had to be asking questions I'd never be done. It ain't for us to ask the reason why. Now, who was it said that? Was it Napoleon, dearie? I've no 'ead for geography."

Despite her dilemma, Pamela could scarcely suppress a smile at the woman's unconscious humour. She was a woman of about fifty, with thin, pinched features—the office cleaner type—a woman who would appear utterly alien to her environment, were she divorced from her pail and mop.

"I really don't know," Pamela said kindly, taking the cup and saucer from the woman's work-stained hand.

The tea revived her almost immediately. Her head ceased to gyrate. She felt her heart beating once again.

"But can't you tell me where I am?" asked the girl plaintively.

"I could, but I daren't," whispered the woman. " 'E'd murder me if I was to talk."

"Who would? Who is he?"

"Lawks a me, young woman," exclaimed the other. "Can't you say anythin' without makin' it a question?"

"I want to know where I am and why I am here," Pamela demanded.

"Easier asked than answered," the woman told her. "A quiet tongue never 'armed no one. There I go again. You with yer questions and me with my quotations. Who was it said that, dearie? It's on the tip of me tongue, but I'm blamed if I can remember."

Pamela had drained the cup and handed it back to the woman. Under any other conditions this woman would have been an enjoyment and an entertainment, but Pamela felt that things were much too serious for quotations or origins.

"Well, dearie, I must be a-goin'. I don't want 'im to be tellin' me orf."

Saying this, the woman opened the door and closed it behind her. Hardly had the door closed than it opened again, and the girl's eyes opened wide with wonder as she saw Delisle crossing the room towards her. He was smiling, but his smile was queer and unnatural.

"Good morning, Pamela, my dear. I hope you have slept well."

The girl sprang from the divan and faced him.

"What is the meaning of this—this outrage?" she demanded imperiously. "I thought—I thought," she ended lamely.

"You thought what, my dear? Thought that you were going to rescue your precious Ian from the clutches of Satan. Is that it?"

Pamela walked back to the divan and sat down. She still felt rather weak from the effects of the drug.

"Will you please stop all this nonsense and tell me the object of this spectacular and very theatrical abduction?"

"I doubt whether one could be charged with abducting one's bride," he leered. Then he went off obliquely. "I'm sorry the place isn't in better order. The truth is I didn't expect you quite so soon."

Pamela had now absolutely no delusions about Rodney Delisle. She was conscious that it was he who was holding Ian a prisoner, and that in some way he had managed either to force Ian to write that letter or else it was a particularly clever forgery. Why had she relied so much on the handwriting? Why had she not trusted her instinct that it was not in Ian's style of English? Ian could write so easily, so well. These villains might forge his handwriting. They could not forge his brains or the personality that was behind his letters.

"How much do you demand this time?"

The girl flung the words at him scornfully.

The shot went home and he coloured. His eyes narrowed just as she had seen them that afternoon at his cottage at Blacon.

"Enough of that," he cried hoarsely, encircling her roughly in his powerful arms. "Enough of that, I say. You need taming, and I'm told I'm an expert at that sort of thing."

She saw his evil face leering above her own and then, for some reason unaccountable to her, she fainted.

Delisle felt her body grow limp in his arms. He still smiled as he laid her with exaggerated reverence on the divan. Then he left the room, locking the door carefully behind him.

At three o'clock that same afternoon the telephone bell tinkled in the hall at Blacon Grange.

John Vance, beside himself with anxiety, rushed towards it.

"Is that Mr. Vance," came a smooth voice.

"Good. This is Delisle at this end. My price has gone up since last we met. It is now five thousand; that is two thousand for withholding information from the police and three thousand for the safe return of your daughter. You heard what I said? Safe return! The money must be paid by midnight tomorrow. It must be sent by registered letter post and in notes. It must be addressed to Monsieur Charles Darracq, 18 Rue de Ste. Pauline, Paris. If you mention this to the police and anything happens I cannot vouch for the safety of your daughter. Let me repeat the address again, and I advise you to write it down. Monsieur Charles Darracq, 18 Rue de Ste. Pauline, Paris."

That was all.

The click of the receiver told Vance that Delisle had hung up.

CHAPTER TWENTY-SEVEN

"WHAT NEWS?"

FOUR HOURS LATER a wildly distracted figure demanded to see Inspector Burke at Scotland Yard.

Burke was, fortunately, in the building and came down to the waiting-room immediately.

He saw a big change in the John Vance who was standing there. The man seemed to have aged by almost ten years since he had seen him at Blacon Grange a few days ago.

The inspector took Vance up to his office and poured him out a stiff whisky, which was kept in the desk for purely medicinal purposes.

It was odd that Vance should have turned up like this because less than an hour ago Sir Michael Kenyon had been insisting on his immediate arrest, and this despite important new evidence which Burke had been able to lay before him. Sir Michael felt that the time had now arrived for action. Public opinion was becoming restive, and the assistant commissioner was rather scared of public opinion, far more scared, in fact, than he was of the Home Secretary himself.

Vance was glad of the stimulant. Burke had already had a somewhat incoherent account of Pamela's disappearance that morning. It had alarmed him—added to his difficulties. Now, here was Vance. But when Vance had told him of his telephone conversation that afternoon with Delisle, Burke's face grew set and serious.

"Isn't it odd, Mr. Burke, that you can't find the man? He must be in London somewhere. Can't you *do* something? Aren't you Scotland Yard? And he's got Pamela!"

"London's quite a big place," Burke reminded the agitated man. "We are doing our best, but you must remember that we are not magicians. Miss Pamela is a most charming young lady. You can rest assured that we'll get her back for you as soon as possible."

After taking particulars of the time of the call Burke gave hurried instructions for the source of that call to be traced. Not that he felt that it would help him. He knew now that Delisle was too cute a customer to give himself away quite so easily.

"I don't know what more we can do," Burke admitted. "We've just got to hope for the best."

. "And in the meantime something may happen to Pamela," burst out Vance indignantly. "She's a casual acquaintance to you, but she's my daughter—my child. Can't you understand? I can't just hope for the best, as you suggest. I must do something. I tell you it won't do—this waiting about, Mr. Burke. . . . I'm going to pay that fellow what he wants. I can't go on like this a moment longer. I must have my child."

"You are forgetting what you said about your informing the police," Burke reminded him.

"How should he know? I ask you, Mr. Burke. How should he know? I don't care what happens so long as Pamela is returned safely to me."

Burke listened patiently.

Then he spoke quietly, yet with the voice of authority: "I don't think you quite realise, Mr. Vance, that Delisle, from information I have acquired during the past forty-eight hours, is the head of a particularly large syndicate of confidence tricksters operating not only in London, but on transatlantic liners and in most of the capitals of Europe. For aught I know his informers may be legion. One of them was probably hanging around on the Embankment as you came along here. Perhaps already Delisle is being informed of your visit to me. What will happen if you pay that money? Delisle will know for a certainty that it is a trap and that you have attempted to double-cross him. No, Mr. Vance, that won't do. I just want you to realise that I have not been so inactive as you may be inclined to believe. At this moment twenty or thirty Special Branch men are scouring the Metropolis and the suburbs for the smallest trace of Delisle. From the moment that order was issued Delisle was a marked man. He dare not leave England. He does not know it, but he is trapped."

For a moment Burke's explanation appeared to pacify John Vance. On the other hand it was all very well for Burke to talk so confidently about Delisle. To John Vance at that moment Delisle was less than nothing. It was his daughter, Pamela, that meant everything; and what was more Burke did not appear to be paying any attention to that aspect of the case.

"I'm sorry, Mr. Burke, if I appeared rude," Vance said, "but I want you to know that Pamela means everything to me; far more in fact than all this tragic business connected with Stone's death. If necessary I would gladly go to the scaffold myself if by so doing I could save her from that blackguard Delisle. And to think I gave him my hospitality," he added bitterly; "to think that I looked on him as a possible suitor for Pamela. God, what a fool I've been!"

"Now, Mr. Vance," said Burke quietly, laying a hand on the elder man's shoulder, "you just get along to your hotel, and in the morning . . . who knows what news we may have for you? And what's more, I don't want you to think I'm forgetting Pamela, but I've been playing around with an idea that Pamela herself may be the means of leading us to Delisle's lair. Mind you, I know nothing definite. It's just an idea, but believe it or not, Mr. Vance, there have been occasions when I've been rather good at ideas."

"I hope you're right, Mr. Burke. If you've any news at all for me I'll be at The Clifton."

When Vance had gone Burke picked up the telephone on his desk and instructed one of his men to see that John Vance reached his hotel in safety. He had long ago decided to take no chances.

He sat down at his desk and gave further instructions for a call to the Prefect of the Paris police in reference to the address Delisle had given. Then methodically he paced up and down his room awaiting Forster.

Forster came in humming a tune—one of the habits he had acquired from Burke himself.

"What news?" asked Burke calmly.

"The car's been found at Wandsworth—close to the Common. It was in a garage there. The proprietor of the place says that a man left it there around midnight last night. From the description I was given I should say that it's our old friend Grainger."

"Any further ideas or reports about that address?" was Burke's next question.

"Only one, and oddly enough I thought of that myself fifteen minutes ago. There's a number of roads around Wandsworth beginning with a 'B,' but none ending with 'h.' Might that not have been a mistake in the spelling?"

"I suppose they're all being combed?"

"You've said it, Chief. What time do we sleep tonight?"

"We don't sleep until we've got Delisle," snapped Burke. "I'm waiting for a call from Paris."

Forster sat down heavily at Burke's desk. He pulled from his pocket a typewritten list of the streets all beginning with the letter 'B' and ending with an 'h.' Most of them had been crossed off. He regarded the list for a few silent moments then he folded it carefully and returned it to his pocket.

On Burke's desk was a volume of the London Street Directory. Carelessly he began to turn the pages of the index. Suddenly he stiffened.

"We've been a brace of ruddy fools," he remarked sourly. "We've been looking for a road in Wandsworth beginning with a 'B' and ending with 'h,' when it doesn't end with 'h' at all. Look!"

Burke ceased his pacing and stopped beside the desk. "There you are," went on Forster, "Bessboro' Road, Wandsworth. Number 8—Mrs. Amy Haggers."

"By jove, Forster, that brain of yours does work after all. Are you ready?"

"My middle name is 'Intelligence,'" smiled Forster, as he struggled awkwardly into his overcoat.

Meanwhile at No. 8 Bessborough Road, Wandsworth, Rodney Delisle had received an important piece of information. He received it on a private wireless installation in the cellar of the house. It was a set for which he held no licence and which was used only in cases of emergency.

The message told him that John Vance had visited Scotland Yard. It told him more than that; it told him that a cordon of police was combing the neighbourhood since the discovery of the car. They were making a house to house search armed with warrants in every road with a name beginning with a letter 'B.'

Delisle picked up a bag he always kept ready packed and, under cover of the darkness, slipped almost casually away into the night.

CHAPTER TWENTY-EIGHT

AN AIR CRASH

DELISLE WALKED RAPIDLY to the small, obscure lock-up garage where he kept his car. Occasionally as he walked he glanced backwards over his shoulder. At first he imagined he was mistaken, but gradually he confirmed the thought that someone was following him. Cautiously he drew aside into a shadow patch beneath some trees. The hurrying figure drew abreast of him. Delisle recognised the lopping walk at once, and he heaved a sigh of immense relief. It was Grainger.

"Where are you going?" hissed Delisle, gripping the man's arm.

"With you, Boss," answered Grainger promptly. "I saw you slip out and I knew that you meant business."

Delisle said nothing. He was telling himself that Grainger would probably come in useful.

"Why should you think I was going?" he asked.

"Instinct, Boss. Besides, there are too many cops around these parts tonight. The air's full of 'em, and I've no mind to meet Forster again."

The pair walked on in silence. Grainger was now dutifully carrying Delisle's suitcase.

Unlocking the door of the garage, Delisle gave a curt instruction and Grainger backed the car out, and it was Grainger who remained at the wheel when the car was finally out in the road.

"Where to?" he asked, although in his own mind he knew what their destination would be.

"Caterham, of course. Where else would we be going?"

"We're not flying tonight?" questioned Grainger in alarm.

"No, we're flying with bells on in the morning," answered Delisle icily.

Grainger decided to say no more. England was growing hourly more unhealthy.

The car sped onwards into the night in a south-easterly direction. Grainger knew every inch of the way. At last the car turned into a side lane off the main road and made its way along the rutty surface for three hundred yards.

Delisle climbed out and opened a gate leading into a field, in which stood a barn-like structure. Grainger had switched off the car's engine and turned off the lights. Then he followed his employer across the field.

More unlocking of doors, and Delisle passed inside. A few moments later both men were towing a light aeroplane out into the night. Delisle climbed into the cockpit and illuminated the instrument panel. He noted with satisfaction that the petrol tank was full and that the oil was adequate. He switched on the ignition, and Grainger, having deposited the luggage in the small closed rear compartment, gave the small light propeller a swing. The engine was cold, and Grainger had to swing her more than once. At last the engine roared as Delisle opened the throttle slightly.

The barn doors closed, Grainger climbed up behind the pilot. Slowly the machine taxied across the uneven ground until that indefinable sense of lightness told them she was rising. The moon had set an hour since and the night sky was gaily perforated with stars. Delisle first thought of turning eastwards and following the twisty outline of the Thames, but on second thoughts he considered such a course might prove dangerous. Better, perhaps, to head due south and strike the coast that way.

The engine was responding beautifully and Delisle was feeling particularly pleased with himself. Not so pleased, of course, as he would have done if his little plan of blackmail against John Vance had been successful.

Grainger had frequently accompanied him on these illicit trips to the Continent. Delisle did not use the legitimate air ports. There was a little place near Chantilly which served its purpose well indeed. The owner had expensive notions, but such foibles had to be patiently borne. It was Delisle's intention to leave the machine at Chantilly and proceed next day to Berlin. Once in the German capital, he would summon a conference of the members of the syndicate and discover what their plans were for the immediate future. Perhaps, while in Berlin, the man whom London and elsewhere knew as Rodney Delisle would cease to exist. His body would be taken from a culvert battered beyond physical recognition, but Rodney Delisle's papers would be in the pocket of the jacket. Of course, Scotland Yard would be informed, and certain very valuable erasions would have to be made in the files of a case which was pending. Later, perhaps, London would greet another personality. The thought tickled his vanity. Life held so many glittering potentialities.

Grainger's eyes were on the steady alert figure in front of him. He admired the cool nerve; the suave discretion; the punctiliousness. But Grainger was conscious of something else. He had flown on many occasions in this reliable British machine. He knew the "feel" of it as well as he did that of the car. They were losing height. He was certain of it. Slowly, but surely. He leaned across to the man in front and pointed a finger that trembled at the altimeter and attracted Delisle's attention to it.

Mechanically but calmly the pilot lifted the little machine's nose a degree. Nothing happened, and a puzzled look crept into Delisle's eyes. He pulled again at the controls. But still the machine was losing altitude.

Panic seized Grainger. He had not the remotest idea where they might be. Below them was a black void—bottomless. Above—an arc sprinkled with diamonds. Then something loomed up dark and forbidding right in front of the machine's nose. Grainger screamed. Delisle sat fascinated by the sight of disaster—inevitable disaster unless the aeroplane stood on her tail and rose vertically into the night sky.

The crash roared in both men's ears. A splash of flame blinded them. For a moment the machine seemed suspended against a rough black curtain. As the plane struck the earth there was a roar followed instantly by a second flash and a burst of crimson flame. . . . Oblivion. . . .

~ ~ ~ ~ ~

Pamela Vance was sleeping when she was aroused by a furious knocking at the door of the room. She sat up, trembling. The room was black and she had no matches to ignite the gas at the jet.

"What do you want?" she called shrilly.

The only answer she got was the sound of someone charging heavily at the door. Came a splintering of wood and a human form tumbled incontinently into the room. The white beam of an electric hand torch swayed drunkenly around the apartment, finally coming to rest on her frightened face.

"It's all right, Miss," came a reassuring voice, and Pamela's heart beat wildly. It was the voice of authority—the police.

A moment later someone struck a match and applied it to the gas-jet. It was then that she saw Inspector Curtis Burke and Sergeant Forster standing in the doorway. Burke came forward. "Are you all right, Miss Vance?" There was a note of anxiety in his voice.

She nodded, scarcely trusting herself to speak.

"Thank God for that," he exclaimed fervently.

A few moments later, while Pamela was getting into her coat, came Ian Grenville. The amazement had not yet died out of his eyes. The relief had come so suddenly that it seemed untrue. The two stood staring at one another unbelieving.

"Pamela!" Ian exclaimed. "What on earth are you doing here?"

"You ought to know; you sent for me to help you, didn't you?" she asked mischievously.

Burke came in to interrupt Grenville's puzzled frown. The police had searched the house from roof to cellar and found no one but Mrs. Haggers, the woman who had been looking after Pamela. She was sobbing hysterically, but at the sight of the girl she struggled out of the grasp of a uniformed constable and rushed across to her.

"Miss! Miss!" she cried. "Don't let 'em send me to prison. I ain't done nothing wrong. 'Onest I haven't."

Pamela turned to Burke, a question in her eyes.

He nodded. "She's not our meat," he acknowledged. "I expect she'll be released after inquiries. Our main quarry seems to have gone. I warned your father, Miss Vance, that he was well served with information."

"Is Daddy in London?" she asked jubilantly.

"He's at the Clifton Hotel at this moment. We'll phone him later with the news. And you, Ian, my lad, you'd better put a call in to Blacon. Sir John may think better of me than he does now.

Ian laughed. It was the first time he had laughed for thirty-six hours, and the experience refreshed him." |

"What's happened to Delisle?" he asked, suddenly releasing Pamela and turning to Burke. "I've a particular score to settle with that. . . ."

Pamela caught him by the arm. "Sh!" she admonished. "I hope you won't forget, Ian, that there are ladies present."

An interruption came with the arrival of Sergeant Forster, utterly disconsolate.

"All gone," he muttered, sadly, "and I did so want to have a chat, Scully." He turned abruptly to Mrs. Haggers. "What time did the boss leave, Amy?"

The woman turned frightened eyes on the sergeant.

"Search me," she exclaimed. "I thought he was 'ere all the time. Bad cess to 'im."

Half an hour later Ian and Pamela were driving back to the West End in Burke's car. Another cordon had been posted in the hopes of catching some of the fugitives, but Burke was not sanguine of success. The kind of men Delisle gathered around him were those who had a dozen or more bolt-holes.

Leaving the girl and Ian at the Clifton Hotel, Burke and Forster went back to the Yard.

Though the night had been a satisfactory one from at least one point of view, the fact that Delisle had managed to get away was a bitter pill for both officers. Burke wanted Delisle. Until he had him the case of Martin Stone could never be closed, and John Vance must still remain under a cloud of suspicion, intangible though it may be.

It was closing up to two-thirty when Burke and Forster were drinking hot coffee in the mess room.

"He can't get out of the country, that's some consolation," muttered Burke between the sips.

"My only hope," said Forster, "is that he doesn't stay at any more houses in roads beginning with a 'B' and ending with an 'h.' "

"Feeling sleepy, Forster?"

"I'm asleep already."

"D'you think we've earned it?"

Forster shook his head. "It's early yet," he surprised Burke by saying. "Another two hours and we'll have beaten the endurance record."

It was said jokingly, and neither knew that both of them were not destined to get any sleep at all that night.

For as they went back upstairs came the news that Inspector Burke was wanted at Reigate.

"Reigate," muttered Burke as he went to the telephone, "now what the blazes. . . ."

"Yes! Inspector Burke speaking. What's that? An air crash. I'll come along right away."

Turning from the instrument, he caught Forster creeping stealthily from the room.

"No, you don't, Forster, my lad. We're wanted. Reigate. There's been an air crash and someone's been taken to Reigate Cottage Hospital badly smashed up."

"They didn't ask specially for me, did they?" Forster inquired dolefully.

"They did not, Forster, but you're coming along all the same."

CHAPTER TWENTY-NINE

CONFESSION

A PLEASANT-FACED night-sister conducted Inspector Burke and Sergeant Forster up to the emergency ward as the clock was striking four.

"Doctor says the poor fellow won't live the night, Inspector. Is he a friend of yours?"

"I don't quite know until I've seen him," Burke told her gently.

"He didn't ask for you specially, of course," she admitted, and Forster cast a pitying look in Burke's direction. "He just kept repeating 'Burke . . . Scotland Yard,' just like that. I thought perhaps he was one of your men."

"Where did the accident happen?" inquired Burke, as they arrived at the door of the dimly-lit ward.

"About three miles away, so I was told. It appears the aeroplane crashed into a row of poplars on the hillside."

The sister moved the screens slightly that surrounded the bed and beckoned to Burke to come closer. She was bending over the bed saying: "Come, now, cheer up! I've brought the friend you were asking for."

Rodney Delisle turned his head very slowly until his eyes rested on the immobile figure of Inspector Burke, and a smile came to his bloodless lips.

"That's a good one, eh, Burke? Friend of mine. God knows why she should have imagined I wanted to see you, but now that you're here you'll do as well as anyone. Hello," he added, "and is that dear old Forster you've brought with you? Poor old Grainger," he rambled on. "Poor devil couldn't get out. Must have been roasted to death. I was lucky—or unlucky, I don't know which. I managed to fall clear before she hit the earth."

Forster withdrew discreetly behind the red-backed screens.

Burke sat down on a chair beside the bed.

"I'm sorry this has happened, Delisle."

"I'll bet you are. You can't take me now, Burke. I've cheated you."

It was patent to Burke that the man was dying, and he knew why Forster had gone out of sight behind the screen. He would be ready with his notebook.

"Nothing you'd like to tell me, Delisle?" Burke's question was put kindly. "Why not get it off your conscience?"

Delisle's eyes were fixed on the inspector's face. "If you think I killed Stone, you're wrong," he said quietly. "You know I didn't." Delisle's voice had lost its note of humour. "Rodgers killed Stone."

"With the dagger you stole for him from Vance's collection at Blacon Grange."

"That's right, Burke. You're a damn smart feller. How did you know?"

"Just guessed," answered Burke. "But why give it to Rodgers?"

"Ah, why? And again, why? Because Rodgers was one of my men. He worked for me just as he did for Stone. The only difference was that my work was outside hours. Listen, Burke, I'll tell you something. You know who I am? I'm Rod Lyle, better known, perhaps, as 'The Con King.' Well you know now," he smiled, with a flash of pride. "It's a secret, Burke, but you're welcome. I was getting desperately hard up. The economic depression, as the newspapers call it, has affected our business something scandalously. Not so many American millionaires coming across, and my overhead charges running on all the time. It just couldn't be done. I had to have money. I knew Vance had plenty, but I'd never been able to get at him before. So I went to Blacon. Palled up with the daughter and all that sort of thing. Then I discovered that Stone had something to do with a Mexican oil swindle. That interested me a lot, because my Old Man had dropped a packet in it. I reckoned that Stone owed me something. But I found he hadn't a bean. Then one day, running through the Old Man's papers, I found a mysterious little document all about some silly secret society that once existed out in Mexico and, would you believe it, Burke? There was Vance among the membership." Delisle paused for a moment, struggling for breath, his face twisted in pain. The sister came forward and gave him a sip of liquid from a medicine glass. He grew easier.

"I read the rules and all that," he continued, almost in a whisper, "and worked out my little plot. I thought that if I could have Rodgers kill Stone and get Vance implicated—so well implicated, mind you, that there was a big chance of his getting arrested, I reckoned I was on velvet. At all costs he'd want to keep the guilty knowledge from his daughter. So I sent him the letter in the approved Mexican style. Before that, of course, I had found that Rodgers had a grudge against Stone and wouldn't mind the opportunity of paying off an old score, so long as I could guarantee him immunity from police inquiry. I did so. Rodgers told me that Stone was making an appointment to meet Vance at his office. What the nature of the business was we never knew. Well, I left the sticky part to Rodgers. You know the rest."

Delisle paused again and closed his eyes. His voice was growing weaker.

"But you spoiled it, Burke, and I'll never forgive you. You spoiled it by going down to Blacon and making your fool inquiries and asking questions at the Grange. If you'd laid off a fortnight I reckon old man Vance would have paid up and everyone would have been happy."

"Why did you kill Rodgers?" Burke's voice was coldly official.

"Because I had to. The little rat was getting too much booze and going about blabbing. He was a danger to himself and to me. He's better off where ever he is."

Another pause.

"Don't you really think it was a foolproof plot—until you hopped in on it?" smiled the dying man, and Burke nodded. It certainly was.

"I feel tired, Burke. I've an idea I'm passing out. Tell Forster he may come out now. I think I'll be able to sign that statement."

Forster came out guiltily and placed a pen in the man's fingers.

"Thank you, Delisle. I'm sorry it's happened like this. Anything I can do for you?"

But Delisle was too exhausted to speak. He shook his head very slowly and closed his eyes.

~ ~ ~ ~ ~

A month later Inspector Curtis Burke was spending a week-end at Blacon Grange at the invitation of John Vance and Pamela.

There had been so much to be done in the meantime clearing up the case that he had not had time to give Vance some of the explanations he had wanted when he had been told of Delisle's confession.

Four of them were seated in the lounge with the curtains snugly drawn and a large fire roaring on the hearth.

"So you see," ended Burke, "Delisle had a marvellous brain for details. It has always seemed to me a pity he did not turn it to better uses."

"It was certainly very clever, Mr. Burke," commented Vance. "Of course, he must have been desperate at the end when he abducted Pamela."

Burke nodded. "That was stupid of him. But it wasn't stupid of him to hold Ian. Ian was impetuous. He thought he was doing a great thing. Perhaps he was. But he made the mistake of not looking around him before he went inside that house and sending me a note to the Yard. In that way I have little doubt but what Delisle would have stood his trial."

"I think it happened for the best," said Pamela seriously. "I should have hated the thought of him standing on the scaffold."

"Don't let's talk about it any more," suggested Ian brightly. "I have an idea that the moon is full tonight and that I'd like to watch it rising over the trees. Come along, Pam."

"Don't forget the old saying about a full moon and madness," Burke called after the pair.

Pamela halted and turned.

"Ian's already told me five times today that he's madly in love with me," she mocked.

The moon was like a golden plaque in the velvety sky as Pamela and Ian stood together on the steps of Blacon Grange.

"I think it's beautiful," sighed the girl.

"I think you are," Ian told her, as he watched the moonlight caress her hair.

THE END

RAMBLE HOUSE's

HARRY STEPHEN KEELER WEBWORK MYSTERIES

(RH) indicates the title is available ONLY in the RAMBLE HOUSE edition

The Ace of Spades Murder
The Affair of the Bottled Deuce (RH)
The Amazing Web
The Barking Clock
Behind That Mask
The Book with the Orange Leaves
The Bottle with the Green Wax Seal
The Box from Japan
The Case of the Canny Killer
The Case of the Crazy Corpse (RH)
The Case of the Flying Hands (RH)
The Case of the Ivory Arrow
The Case of the Jeweled Ragpicker
The Case of the Lavender Gripsack
The Case of the Mysterious Moll
The Case of the 16 Beans
The Case of the Transparent Nude (RH)
The Case of the Transposed Legs
The Case of the Two-Headed Idiot (RH)
The Case of the Two Strange Ladies
The Circus Stealers (RH)
Cleopatra's Tears
A Copy of Beowulf (RH)
The Crimson Cube (RH)
The Face of the Man From Saturn
Find the Clock
The Five Silver Buddhas
The 4th King
The Gallows Waits, My Lord! (RH)
The Green Jade Hand
Finger! Finger!
Hangman's Nights (RH)
I, Chameleon (RH)
I Killed Lincoln at 10:13! (RH)
The Iron Ring
The Man Who Changed His Skin (RH)
The Man with the Crimson Box
The Man with the Magic Eardrums
The Man with the Wooden Spectacles
The Marceau Case
The Matilda Hunter Murder
The Monocled Monster

The Murder of London Lew
The Murdered Mathematician
The Mysterious Card (RH)
The Mysterious Ivory Ball of Wong
    Shing Li (RH)
The Mystery of the Fiddling Cracks-
man
The Peacock Fan
The Photo of Lady X (RH)
The Portrait of Jirjohn Cobb
Report on Vanessa Hewstone (RH)
Riddle of the Travelling Skull
Riddle of the Wooden Parrakeet (RH)
The Scarlet Mummy (RH)
The Search for X-Y-Z
The Sharkskin Book
Sing Sing Nights
The Six From Nowhere (RH)
The Skull of the Waltzing Clown
The Spectacles of Mr. Cagliostro
Stand By—London Calling!
The Steeltown Strangler
The Stolen Gravestone (RH)
Strange Journey (RH)
The Strange Will
The Straw Hat Murders (RH)
The Street of 1000 Eyes (RH)
Thieves' Nights
Three Novellos (RH)
The Tiger Snake
The Trap (RH)
Vagabond Nights (Defrauded Yegg-
man)
Vagabond Nights 2 (10 Hours)
The Vanishing Gold Truck
The Voice of the Seven Sparrows
The Washington Square Enigma
When Thief Meets Thief
The White Circle (RH)
The Wonderful Scheme of Mr. Chris-
    topher Thorne
X. Jones—of Scotland Yard
Y. Cheung, Business Detective

Keeler Related Works

A To Izzard: A Harry Stephen Keeler Companion by Fender Tucker—Articles and stories about Harry, by Harry, and in his style. Included is a compleat bibliography.

Wild About Harry: Reviews of Keeler Novels—Edited by Richard Polt & Fender Tucker—22 reviews of works by Harry Stephen Keeler from *Keeler News*. A perfect introduction to the author.

The Keeler Keyhole Collection: Annotated newsletter rants from Harry Stephen Keeler, edited by Francis M. Nevins. Over 400 pages of incredibly personal Keeleriana.

Fakealoo—Pastiches of the style of Harry Stephen Keeler by selected demented members of the HSK Society. Updated every year with the new winner.

Strands of the Web: Short Stories of Harry Stephen Keeler—29 stories, just about all that Keeler wrote, are edited and introduced by Fred Cleaver.

RAMBLE HOUSE's LOON SANCTUARY

A Clear Path to Cross—Sharon Knowles short mystery stories by Ed Lynskey.

A Corpse Walks in Brooklyn and Other Stories—Volume 5 in the Day Keene in the Detective Pulps series.

A Fair Californian—Novel by Olive Harper about a young woman's quest for gold — a quest that turns into something completely unexpected.

A Jimmy Starr Omnibus—Three 40s novels by Jimmy Starr.

A Niche in Time and Other Stories—Classic SF by William F. Temple.

A Shot Rang Out—Three decades of reviews and articles by today's Anthony Boucher, Jon Breen. An essential book for any mystery lover's library.

A Snark Selection—Lewis Carroll's *The Hunting of the Snark* with two Snarkian chapters by Harry Stephen Keeler—Illustrated by Gavin L. O'Keefe.

A Young Man's Heart—A forgotten early classic by Cornell Woolrich.

Alexander Laing Novels—*The Motives of Nicholas Holtz* and *Dr. Scarlett*, stories of medical mayhem and intrigue from the 30s.

An Angel in the Street—Modern hardboiled noir by Peter Genovese.

Automaton—Brilliant treatise on robotics: 1928-style! By H. Stafford Hatfield.

Away From the Here and Now—Clare Winger Harris stories, collected by Richard A. Lupoff

Beast or Man?—A 1930 novel of racism and horror by Sean M'Guire. Introduced by John Pelan.

Black Beadle—A 1939 thriller by E.C.R. Lorac.

Black Hogan Strikes Again—Australia's Peter Renwick pens a tale of the 30s outback.

Black River Falls—Suspense from the master, Ed Gorman.

Blondy's Boy Friend—A snappy 1930 story by Philip Wylie, writing as Leatrice Homesley.

Blood in a Snap—The *Finnegan's Wake* of the 21st century, by Jim Weiler.

Blood Moon—The first of the Robert Payne series by Ed Gorman.

Bogart '48—Hollywood action with Bogie by John Stanley and Kenn Davis

Butterfly Man—1930s novel by Lew Levenson about a dancer who must come to terms with his homosexuality.

Calling Lou Largo!—Two Lou Largo novels by William Ard.

Cathedral of Horror—First volume of collected stories by weird fiction writer Arthur J. Burks.

Chalk Face—Curious supernatural murder thriller by Waldo Frank.

Cornucopia of Crime—Francis M. Nevins assembled this huge collection of his writings about crime literature and the people who write it. Essential for any serious mystery library.

Corpse Without Flesh—Strange novel of forensics by George Bruce

Crimson Clown Novels—By Johnston McCulley, author of the Zorro novels, *The Crimson Clown* and *The Crimson Clown Again.*

Dago Red—22 tales of dark suspense by Bill Pronzini.

Dark Sanctuary—Weird Menace story by H. B. Gregory.

David Hume Novels—*Corpses Never Argue, Cemetery First Stop, Make Way for the Mourners, Eternity Here I Come.* 1930s British hardboiled fiction with an attitude.

David&Son: Peregrine Parentus and other tales—Collection of tales and memoirs by Avram Davidson and Ethan Davidson, some published for the first time. Introduced by Grania Davidson Davis.

Dead Man Talks Too Much—Hollywood boozer by Weed Dickenson.

Death in a Bowl—1930's murder mystery by Raoul Whitfield.

Death March of the Dancing Dolls and Other Stories—Volume Three in the Day Keene in the Detective Pulps series. Introduced by Bill Crider.

Deep Space and other Stories—A collection of SF gems by Richard A. Lupoff.

Detective Duff Unravels It—Episodic mysteries by Harvey O'Higgins.

Devil's Planet—Locked room mystery set on the planet Mars, by Manly Wade Wellman.

Dime Novels: Ramble House's 10-Cent Books—*Knife in the Dark* by Robert Leslie Bellem, *Hot Lead* and *Song of Death* by Ed Earl Repp, *A Hashish House in New York* by H.H. Kane, and five more.

Doctor Arnoldi—Tiffany Thayer's story of the death of death.

Don Diablo: Book of a Lost Film—Two-volume treatment of a western by Paul Landres, with diagrams. Intro by Francis M. Nevins.

Dope and Swastikas—Two strange novels from 1922 by Edmund Snell

Dope Tales #1—Two dope-riddled classics; *Dope Runners* by Gerald Grantham and *Death Takes the Joystick* by Phillip Condé.

Dope Tales #2—Two more narco-classics; *The Invisible Hand* by Rex Dark and *The Smokers of Hashish* by Norman Berrow.

Dope Tales #3—Two enchanting novels of opium by the master, Sax Rohmer. *Dope* and *The Yellow Claw.*

Double Hot & Double Sex—Two combos of '60s softcore sex novels by Morris Hershman.

Dr. Odin—Douglas Newton's 1933 racial potboiler comes back to life.

E. Charles Vivian—*Evidence in Blue, Accessory After* and *The Lady of the Terraces.*

E.C.R. Lorac—*Black Beadle, The Case in the Clinic, The Devil and the C.I.D.* and *Slippery Staircase.*

E. R. Punshon novels—*Information Received, Crossword Mystery, Dictator's Way, Diabolic Candelabra, Music Tells All, Helen Passes By, The House of Godwinsson, The Golden Dagger, The Attending Truth, Strange Ending, Brought to Light, Dark is the Clue, Triple Quest,* and *Six Were Present*: featuring Bobby Owen.

Ed "Strangler" Lewis: Facts within a Myth—Authoritative illustrated biography of the famous American wrestler Ed Lewis, by noted historian Steve Yohe.

Evangelical Cockroach—Jack Woodford writes about writing.

Fatal Accident—1936 murder-by-automobile mystery by Cecil M. Wills.

Fighting Mad—Todd Robbins' 1922 novel about boxing and life

Five Million in Cash—Gangster thriller by Tiffany Thayer writing as O. B. King.

Food for the Fungus Lady—Collection of weird stories by Ralston Shields, edited and introduced by John Pelan.

Francis M. Nevins—Three omnibus volumes of novels: *Publish and Perish / Corrupt and Ensnare, Into the Same River Twice / Beneficiaries' Requiem* and *The 120-Hour Clock / The Ninety Million Dollar Mouse*.

Freaks and Fantasies—Eerie tales by Tod Robbins, collaborator of Tod Browning on the film FREAKS.

Gadsby—A lipogram (a novel without the letter E). Ernest Vincent Wright's last work, published in 1939 right before his death.

Gelett Burgess Novels—*The Master of Mysteries, The White Cat, Two O'Clock Courage, Ladies in Boxes, Find the Woman, The Heart Line, The Picaroons* and *Lady Mechante*. Recently added is A Gelett Burgess Sampler, edited by Alfred Jan. All are introduced by Richard A. Lupoff.

Geronimo—S. M. Barrett's 1905 autobiography of a noble American.

Gordon Eklund—*Second Creation, Retro Man* and *Stalking the Sun*: three volumes of the author's best short stories.

Go Forth and Multiply—Anthology of science fiction tales of repopulation, edited by Gordon Van Gelder.

Hake Talbot Novels—*Rim of the Pit, The Hangman's Handyman*. Classic locked room mysteries, with mapback covers by Gavin O'Keefe.

Hands Out of Hell and Other Stories—John H. Knox's eerie hallucinations

Hell is a City—William Ard's masterpiece.

Hollywood Dreams—A novel of Tinsel Town and the Depression by Richard O'Brien.

Homicide House—#6 in the Day Keene in the Detective Pulps series.

Hostesses in Hell and Other Stories—Russell Gray's most graphic stories

House of the Restless Dead—Strange and ominous tales by Hugh B. Cave

Inclination to Murder—1966 thriller by New Zealand's Harriet Hunter.

Invaders from the Dark—Classic werewolf tale from Greye La Spina.

J. Poindexter, Colored—Classic satirical black novel by Irvin S. Cobb.

Jack Mann Novels—Strange murder in the English countryside. *Gees' First Case, Nightmare Farm, Grey Shapes, The Ninth Life, The Glass Too Many, Her Ways Are Death, The Kleinert Case* and *Maker of Shadows*.

Jake Hardy—A lusty western tale from Wesley Tallant.

James Corbett—*Vampire of the Skies, The Ghost Plane, Murder Begets Murder* and *The Air Killer* – strange thriller novels from this singular British author.

Jim Harmon Double Novels—*Vixen Hollow/Celluloid Scandal, The Man Who Made Maniacs/Silent Siren, Ape Rape/Wanton Witch, Sex Burns Like Fire/Twist Session, Sudden Lust/Passion Strip, Sin Unlimited/Harlot Master, Twilight Girls/Sex Institution*. Written in the early 60s and never reprinted until now.

Joel Townsley Rogers Novels and Short Stories—By the author of *The Red Right Hand: Once In a Red Moon, Lady With the Dice, The Stopped Clock, Never Leave My Bed*. Also two short story collections: *Night of Horror* and *Killing Time*.

John Carstairs, Space Detective—Arboreal Sci-fi by Frank Belknap Long

John G. Brandon—*The Case of the Withered Hand, Finger-Prints Never Lie*, and *Death on Delivery*: crime thrillers by Australian author John G. Brandon.

John S. Glasby—Two collections of Glasby's Lovecraftian stories: *The Brooding City* and *Beyond the Rim*. Introduced by John Pelan.

Joseph Shallit Novels—*The Case of the Billion Dollar Body, Lady Don't Die on My Doorstep, Kiss the Killer, Yell Bloody Murder, Take Your Last Look*. One of America's best 50's authors and a favorite of author Bill Pronzini.

Keller Memento—45 short stories of the amazing and weird by Dr. David Keller.

Killer's Caress—Cary Moran's 1936 hardboiled thriller.

Knight Asrael and Other Stories—Collection of fourteen fantasy tales by Una Ashworth Taylor

Knowing the Unknowable: Putting Psi to Work—Damien Broderick, PhD puts forward the valid case for evidence of Psi.

Lady of the Yellow Death and Other Stories—More stories by Wyatt Blassingame.

Laughing Death—1932 Yellow Peril thriller by Walter C. Brown.

League of the Grateful Dead and Other Stories—Volume One in the Day Keene in the Detective Pulps series.

Library of Death—Ghastly tale by Ronald S. L. Harding, introduced by John Pelan

Lords of the Earth—A novel of meddling dabblers in the occult invoking the ancient powers of Atlantis. J.M.A. Mills' sequel to *The Tomb of the Dark Ones*.

Mad-Doctor Merciful—Collin Brooks' unsettling novel of medical experimentation with supernatural forces.

Malcolm Jameson Novels and Short Stories—*Astonishing! Astounding!, Tarnished Bomb, The Alien Envoy and Other Stories* and *The Chariots of San Fernando and Other Stories*. All introduced and edited by John Pelan or Richard A. Lupoff.

Man Out of Hell and Other Stories—Volume II of the John H. Knox weird pulps collection.

Marblehead: A Novel of H.P. Lovecraft—A long-lost masterpiece from Richard A. Lupoff. This is the "director's cut", the long version that has never been published before.

Mark of the Laughing Death and Other Stories—Shockers from the pulps by Francis James, introduced by John Pelan.

Mark Hansom Novels—*Master of Souls, The Ghost of Gaston Revere, The Madman, The Shadow on the House, Sorcerer's Chessmen* & *The Wizard of Berner's Abbey*.

Max Afford Novels—*Owl of Darkness, Death's Mannikins, Blood on His Hands, The Dead Are Blind, The Sheep and the Wolves, Sinners in Paradise* and *Two Locked Room Mysteries and a Ripping Yarn* by one of Australia's finest mystery novelists.

Miles Burton novels — *A Smell of Smoke, Death Leaves No Card, Situation Vacant* and *Death Paints a Picture*.

Mistress of Terror—Fourth volume of the collected weird tales of Wyatt Blassingame.

Molly and her Man of War— Romantic novel with a difference, by Arabella Kenealy.

Money Brawl—Two books about the writing business by Jack Woodford and H. Bedford-Jones. Introduced by Richard A. Lupoff.

More Secret Adventures of Sherlock Holmes—Gary Lovisi's second collection of tales about the unknown sides of the great detective.

Muddled Mind: Complete Works of Ed Wood, Jr.—David Hayes and Hayden Davis deconstruct the life and works of the mad, but canny, genius.

Murder among the Nudists—1934 mystery by Peter Hunt, featuring a naked Detective-Inspector going undercover in a nudist colony.

Murder in Black and White—1931 classic tennis whodunit by Evelyn Elder.

Murder in Shawnee—Two novels of the Alleghenies by John Douglas: *Shawnee Alley Fire* and *Haunts*.

Murder in Suffolk—A 1938 murder mystery novel by the mysterious 'A. Fielding.'

My Deadly Angel—1955 Cold War drama by John Chelton.

My First Time: The One Experience You Never Forget—Michael Birchwood—64 true first-person narratives of how they lost it.

My Touch Brings Death—Second volume of collected stories by Russell Gray.

Mysterious Martin, the Master of Murder—Two versions of a strange 1912 novel by Tod Robbins about a man who writes books that can kill.

Norman Berrow Novels—*The Bishop's Sword, Ghost House, Don't Go Out After Dark, Claws of the Cougar, The Smokers of Hashish, The Secret Dancer, Don't Jump Mr. Boland!, The Footprints of Satan, Fingers for Ransom, The Three Tiers of Fantasy, The Spaniard's Thumb, The Eleventh Plague, Words Have Wings, One Thrilling Night, The Lady's in Danger, It Howls at Night, The Terror in the Fog, Oil Under the Window, Murder in the Melody, The Singing Room.* This is the complete Norman Berrow library of locked-room mysteries, several of which are masterpieces.

Old Faithful and Other Stories—SF classic tales by Raymond Z. Gallun

Old Times' Sake—Short stories by James Reasoner from Mike Shayne Magazine.

One Dreadful Night—A classic mystery by Ronald S. L. Harding

Pair O' Jacks—A mystery novel and a diatribe about publishing by Jack Woodford

Pawns of Destiny—Psychological drama by Kay Seaton.

Perfect .38—Two early Timothy Dane novels by William Ard. More to come.

Prince Pax—Devilish intrigue by George Sylvester Viereck and Philip Eldridge

Prose Bowl—Futuristic satire of a world where hack writing has replaced football as our national obsession, by Bill Pronzini and Barry N. Malzberg.

Ralph Trevor—*Murder in Silk, Easy for the Crook, Front Page Murder, The Deputy Avenger, The Phantom Raider* and *Invitation to Murder*.

Red Light—The history of legal prostitution in Shreveport Louisiana by Eric Brock. Includes wonderful photos of the houses and the ladies.

Researching American-Made Toy Soldiers—A 276-page collection of a lifetime of articles by toy soldier expert Richard O'Brien.

Reunion in Hell—Volume One of the John H. Knox series of weird stories from the pulps. Introduced by horror expert John Pelan.

Ripped from the Headlines!—The Jack the Ripper story as told in the newspaper articles in the *New York* and *London Times*.

Rough Cut & New, Improved Murder—Ed Gorman's first two novels.

R. R. Ryan Novels — *Freak Museum, The Subjugated Beast, Death of a Sadist, Echo of a Curse, Devil's Shelter* and *No Escape*. Introduced by John Pelan.

Roland Daniel Novels — *Ruby of a Thousand Dreams, The Girl in the Dark,* and *A Roland Daniel Double: The Signal and The Return of Wu Fang.*

Ruled By Radio — 1925 futuristic novel by Robert L. Hadfield & Frank E. Farncombe.

Rupert Penny Novels — *Policeman's Holiday, Policeman's Evidence, Lucky Policeman, Policeman in Armour, Sealed Room Murder, Sweet Poison, The Talkative Policeman, She had to Have Gas* and *Cut and Run* (by Martin Tanner.) Rupert Penny is the pseudonym of Australian Charles Thornett, a master of the locked room, impossible crime plot.

Sacred Locomotive Flies — Richard A. Lupoff's psychedelic SF story.

Sam — Early gay novel by Lonnie Coleman.

Sand's Game — Spectacular hardboiled noir from Ennis Willie, edited by Lynn Myers and Stephen Mertz, with contributions from Max Allan Collins, Bill Crider, Wayne Dundee, Bill Pronzini, Gary Lovisi and James Reasoner.

Sand's War — More violent fiction from the typewriter of Ennis Willie

Satan's Den Exposed — True crime in Truth or Consequences New Mexico — Award-winning journalism by the *Desert Journal.*

Satan's Secret and Selected Stories — Barnard Stacey's only novel with a selection of his best short stories.

Satans of Saturn — Novellas from the pulps by Otis Adelbert Kline and E. H. Price

Satan's Sin House and Other Stories — Horrific gore by Wayne Rogers

Second Creation — The first volume of selected short stories by Gordon Eklund.

Secrets of a Teenage Superhero — Graphic lit by Jonathan Sweet

Sex Slave — Potboiler of lust in the days of Cleopatra by Dion Leclerq, 1966.

Slammer Days — Two full-length prison memoirs: *Men into Beasts* (1952) by George Sylvester Viereck and *Home Away From Home* (1962) by Jack Woodford.

Star Griffin — Michael Kurland's 1987 masterpiece of SF drollery is back.

Stakeout on Millennium Drive — Award-winning Indianapolis Noir by Ian Woollen.

Strands of the Web: Short Stories of Harry Stephen Keeler — Edited and Introduced by Fred Cleaver.

Summer Camp for Corpses and Other Stories — Weird Menace tales from Arthur Leo Zagat; introduced by John Pelan.

Suzy — A collection of comic strips by Richard O'Brien and Bob Vojtko from 1970.

Tail of the Lizard King / Kaliwood — Two novellas by Adam Mudman Bezecny paying homage to the sleaze genre.

Tales of the Macabre and Ordinary — Modern twisted horror by Chris Mikul, author of the *Bizarrism* series.

Tales of Terror and Torment Vols. #1 & #2 — John Pelan selects and introduces these samplers of weird menace tales from the pulps.

Tenebrae — Ernest G. Henham's 1898 horror tale brought back.

The Alice Books — Lewis Carroll's classics *Alice's Adventures in Wonderland* and *Through the Looking-Glass* together in one volume, with new illustrations by O'Keefe.

The Amorous Intrigues & Adventures of Aaron Burr — by Anonymous. Hot historical action about the man who almost became Emperor of Mexico.

The Anthony Boucher Chronicles — edited by Francis M. Nevins. Book reviews by Anthony Boucher written for the *San Francisco Chronicle,* 1942 – 1947. Essential and fascinating reading by the best book reviewer there ever was.

The Barclay Catalogs — Two essential books about toy soldier collecting by Richard O'Brien

The Basil Wells Omnibus — A collection of Wells' stories by Richard A. Lupoff

The Beautiful Dead and Other Stories — Dreadful tales from Donald Dale

The Best of 10-Story Book — edited by Chris Mikul, over 35 stories from the literary magazine Harry Stephen Keeler edited.

The Bitch Wall — Novel about American soldiers in the Vietnam War, based on Dennis Lane's experiences.

The Black Dark Murders — Vintage 50s college murder yarn by Milt Ozaki, writing as Robert O. Saber.

The Book of Time — The classic novel by H.G. Wells is joined by sequels by Wells himself and three stories by Richard A. Lupoff. Illustrated by Gavin L. O'Keefe.

The Broken Fang and Other Experiences of a Specialist in Spooks — Eerie mystery tales by Uel Key.

The Strange Case of the Antlered Man — A mystery of superstition by Edwy Searles Brooks.

The Case of the Bearded Bride — #4 in the Day Keene in the Detective Pulps series.

The Case of the Little Green Men — Mack Reynolds wrote this love song to sci-fi fans back in 1951 and it's now back in print.

The Charlie Chaplin Murder Mystery — A 2004 tribute by noted film scholar, Wes D. Gehring.

The Cloudbuilders and Other Stories — SF tales from Colin Kapp.

The Collected Writings — Collection of science fiction stories, memoirs and poetry by Carol Carr. Introduction by Karen Haber.

The Compleat Calhoon — All of Fender Tucker's works: Includes *Totah Six-Pack, Weed, Women and Song* and *Tales from the Tower,* plus a CD of all of his songs.

The Compleat Ova Hamlet — Parodies of SF authors by Richard A. Lupoff. This is a brand new edition with more stories and more illustrations by Trina Robbins.

The Contested Earth and Other SF Stories — A never-before published space opera and seven short stories by Jim Harmon.

The Corpse Factory — More horror stories by Arthur Leo Zagat.

The Crackpot and Other Twisted Tales of Greedy Fans and Collectors — The first retrospective collection of the whacky stories of John E. Stockman. Edited by Dwight R. Decker.

The Crimson Butterfly — Early novel by Edmund Snell involving superstition and aberrant Lepidoptera in Borneo.

The Crimson Query — A 1929 thriller from Arlton Eadie. A perfect way to get introduced.

The Daymakers, **City of the Tiger** & **Perchance to Wake** — Three volumes of stories taken from the influential British science fiction magazine *Science Fantasy*. Compiled by John Boston & Damien Broderick.

The Devil Drives — An odd prison and lost treasure novel from 1932 by Virgil Markham.

The Devil of Pei-Ling — Herbert Asbury's 1929 tale of the occult.

The Devil's Mistress — A 1915 Scottish gothic tale by J. W. Brodie-Innes, a member of Aleister Crowley's Golden Dawn.

The Devil's Nightclub and Other Stories — John Pelan introduces some gruesome tales by Nat Schachner.

The Disentanglers — Episodic intrigue at the turn of last century by Andrew Lang

The Dog Poker Code — A spoof of *The Da Vinci Code* by D. B. Smithee.

The Dumpling — Political murder from 1907 by Coulson Kernahan.

The End of It All and Other Stories — Ed Gorman selected his favorite short stories for this huge collection.

The Evil of Li-Sin — A Gerald Verner double, combining *The Menace of Li-Sin* and *The Vengeance of Li-Sin*, together with an introduction by John Pelan and an afterword and bibliography by Chris Verner.

The Fangs of Suet Pudding — A 1944 novel of the German invasion by Adams Farr

The Finger of Destiny and Other Stories — Edmund Snell's superb collection of weird stories of Borneo.

The Gold Star Line — Seaboard adventure from L.T. Reade and Robert Eustace.

The Great Orme Terror — Horror stories by Garnett Radcliffe from the pulps

The Hairbreadth Escapes of Major Mendax — Francis Blake Crofton's 1889 boys' book.

The House That Time Forgot and Other Stories — Insane pulpitude by Robert F. Young

The House of the Vampire — 1907 poetic thriller by George S. Viereck.

The Illustrious Corpse — Murder hijinx from Tiffany Thayer

The Incredible Adventures of Rowland Hern — Intriguing 1928 impossible crimes by Nicholas Olde.

The John Dickson Carr Companion — Comprehensive reference work compiled by James E. Keirans. Indispensable resource for the Carr *aficionado*.

The Julius Caesar Murder Case — A 1935 retelling of the assassination by Wallace Irwin that's more fun than Shakespeare's version.

The Kid Was a Killer — Caryl Chessman's only novel, based on his own experiences.

The Koky Comics — A collection of all of the 1978-1981 Sunday and daily comic strips by Richard O'Brien and Mort Gerberg, in two volumes.

The Lady of the Fjords — Barnard Balogh's novel of Norse gods and heroes, reincarnation, and a love affair transcending mortality.

The Lord of Terror — 1925 mystery with master-criminal, Fantômas.

The Man who was Murdered Twice — Intriguing murder mystery by Robert H. Leitfred.

The Melamare Mystery — A classic 1929 Arsene Lupin mystery by Maurice Leblanc

The Man Who Was Secrett — Epic SF stories from John Brunner

The Man Without a Planet — Science fiction tales by Richard Wilson

The N. R. De Mexico Novels — Robert Bragg, the real N.R. de Mexico, presents *Marijuana Girl, Madman on a Drum, Private Chauffeur* in one volume.

The Night Remembers — A 1991 Jack Walsh mystery from Ed Gorman.

The One After Snelling — Kickass modern noir from Richard O'Brien.

The Organ Reader — A huge compilation of just about everything published in the 1971-1972 radical bay-area newspaper, *THE ORGAN*. A coffee table book that points out the shallowness of the coffee table mindset.

The Place of Hairy Death — Collected weird horror tales by Anthony M. Rud.

The Poker Club — Three in one! Ed Gorman's ground-breaking novel, the short story it was based upon, and the screenplay of the film made from it.

The Private Journal & Diary of John H. Surratt — The memoirs of the man who conspired to assassinate President Lincoln.

The Ramble House Coloring Book — Twenty illustrations to color in, each adapted from one of Gavin L. O'Keefe's cover designs.

The Ramble House Mapbacks — Recently revised book by Gavin L. O'Keefe with color pictures of all the Ramble House books with mapbacks.

The Secret Adventures of Sherlock Holmes — Three Sherlockian pastiches by the Brooklyn author/publisher, Gary Lovisi.

The Secret of the Morgue — Frederick G. Eberhard's 1932 mystery involving murder and forensic science with an undercurrent of the malaise that's driven by Prohibition.

The Sign of the Scorpion — A 1935 Edmund Snell tale of oriental evil.

The Silent Terror of Chu-Sheng — Yellow Peril suspense novel by Eugene Thomas.

The Singular Problem of the Stygian House-Boat — Two classic tales by John Kendrick Bangs about the denizens of Hades.

The Smiling Corpse — Philip Wylie and Bernard Bergman's odd 1935 novel.

The Sorcery Club — Classic supernatural novel by Elliott O'Donnell.

The Spider: Satan's Murder Machines — A thesis about Iron Man.

The Stench of Death: An Odoriferous Omnibus by Jack Moskovitz — Two complete novels and two novellas from 60's sleaze author, Jack Moskovitz.

The Story Writer and Other Stories — Classic SF from Richard Wilson

The Strange Thirteen — Richard B. Gamon's odd stories about Raj India.

The Technique of the Mystery Story — Carolyn Wells' tips about writing.

The Tell-Tale Soul — Two novellas by Bram Stoker Award-winning author Christopher Conlon. Introduction by John Pelan.

The Threat of Nostalgia — A collection of his most obscure stories by Jon Breen

The Time Armada — Fox B. Holden's 1953 SF gem.

The Tomb of the Dark Ones — Adventure in Egypt where ancient forces are roused from æons of slumber. A J. M. A. Mills novel from 1937.

The Tongueless Horror and Other Stories — Volume One of the series of short stories from the weird pulps by Wyatt Blassingame.

The Town from Planet Five — From Richard Wilson, two SF classics, *And Then the Town Took Off* and *The Girls from Planet 5*

The Tracer of Lost Persons — From 1906, an episodic novel that became a hit radio series in the 30s. Introduced by Richard A. Lupoff.

The Trail of the Cloven Hoof — Diabolical horror from 1935 by Arlton Eadie. Introduced by John Pelan.

The Triune Man — Mindscrambling science fiction from Richard A. Lupoff.

The Unholy Goddess and Other Stories — Wyatt Blassingame's first DTP compilation

The Universal Holmes — Richard A. Lupoff's 2007 collection of five Holmesian pastiches and a recipe for giant rat stew.

The Werewolf vs the Vampire Woman — Hard to believe ultraviolence by either Arthur M. Scarm or Arthur M. Scram.

The Whistling Ancestors — A 1936 classic of weirdness by Richard E. Goddard and introduced by John Pelan.

The White Owl — A vintage thriller from Edmund Snell

The White Peril in the Far East — Sidney Lewis Gulick's 1905 indictment of the West and assurance that Japan would never attack the U.S.

The Wonderful Wizard of Oz — by L. Frank Baum and illustrated by Gavin L. O'Keefe.

The Yu-Chi Stone — Novel of intrigue and superstition set in Borneo, by Edmund Snell.

They Called the Shots — Collection of authoritative articles by Francis M. Nevins exploring the action movie directors of the late silents through to the late 1960s.

Time Line — Ramble House artist Gavin O'Keefe selects his most evocative art inspired by the twisted literature he reads and designs.

Tiresias — Psychotic modern horror novel by Jonathan M. Sweet.

Tortures and Towers — Two novellas of terror by Dexter Dayle.

Totah Six-Pack — Fender Tucker's six tales about Farmington in one sleek volume.

Tree of Life, Book of Death — Grania Davis' book of her life.

Trail of the Spirit Warrior — Roger Haley's saga of life in the Indian Territories.

Twelve Who Were Damned — Collection of weird menace tales by Paul Ernst.

Two Kinds of Bad — Two 50s novels by William Ard about Danny Fontaine

Two Suns of Morcali and Other Stories — Evelyn E. Smith's SF tour-de-force

Two-Timers — Time travel double: *The Man Who Mastered Time* by Ray Cummings and *Time Column* and *Taa the Terrible* by Malcolm Jameson. Introduced by Richard A. Lupoff.

Ultra-Boiled — 23 gut-wrenching tales by our Man in Brooklyn, Gary Lovisi.

Up Front From Behind — A 2011 satire of Wall Street by James B. Kobak.

Victims & Villains — Intriguing Sherlockiana from Derham Groves.

Wade Wright Novels — *Echo of Fear, Death At Nostalgia Street, It Leads to Murder* and *Shadows' Edge*, a double book featuring *Shadows Don't Bleed* and *The Sharp Edge*.

Walter S. Masterman Novels — *The Green Toad, The Flying Beast, The Yellow Mistletoe, The Wrong Verdict, The Perjured Alibi, The Border Line, The Bloodhounds Bay, The Curse of Cantire, The Baddington Horror, Death Turns Traitor, The Wrong Letter* and *The Curse of the Reckaviles.* Masterman wrote horror and mystery novels, some introduced by John Pelan.

We Are the Dead and Other Stories — Volume Two in the Day Keene in the Detective Pulps series, introduced by Ed Gorman. When done, there may be 11 in the series.

Welsh Rarebit Tales — Charming stories from 1902 by Harle Oren Cummins

West Texas War and Other Western Stories — Western hijinks by Gary Lovisi.

What Was That?—Ghostly murder mystery from 1920 by Katharine Haviland Taylor.

What If? Volume 3 — Richard A. Lupoff introduces SF short stories that should have won a Hugo, but didn't.

When the Bat Man Thirsts and Other Stories — Weird tales from Frederick C. Davis.

When the Dead Walk — Gary Lovisi takes us into the zombie-infested South.

Whip Dodge: Man Hunter — Wesley Tallant's saga of a bounty hunter of the old West.

Win, Place and Die! — The first new mystery by Milt Ozaki in decades. The ultimate novel of 70s Reno.

Writer, Volumes 1, 2 & 3 — A *magnus opus* from Richard A. Lupoff summing up his life as writer.

You'll Die Laughing — Bruce Elliott's 1945 novel of murder at a practical joker's English countryside manor.

You're Not Alone: 30 Science Fiction Stories from *Cosmos Magazine*, edited by Damien Broderick.

RAMBLE HOUSE
www.ramblehouse.com
flyingspiderster@gmail.com
10329 Sheephead Drive, Vancleave MS 39565 USA

I *always look for* the 'RAMBLE HOUSE' *when I want a* PLEASANT BOOK*!*

Your troubles are at an end when you choose a Ramble House novel. No more doubts! No more disappointments! A Ramble House novel will give you hours of happy reading. Next time, just say to your librarian, "A Ramble House, please!"